John Ruskin

St. Mark's Rest

The History of Venice

John Ruskin

St. Mark's Rest
The History of Venice

ISBN/EAN: 9783337326364

Printed in Europe, USA, Canada, Australia, Japan

Cover: Foto ©Andreas Hilbeck / pixelio.de

More available books at **www.hansebooks.com**

ST. MARK'S REST.

THE HISTORY OF VENICE

WRITTEN FOR THE HELP OF THE FEW TRAVELLERS WHO STILL CARE FOR HER MONUMENTS.

BY

JOHN RUSKIN, LL.D.,

HONORARY STUDENT OF CHRIST CHURCH, AND SLADE PROFESSOR OF FINE ART, OXFORD.

NEW YORK:
JOHN WILEY & SONS,
53 EAST TENTH STREET.
1890.

PREFACE.

GREAT nations write their autobiographies in three manuscripts—the book of their deeds, the book of their words, and the book of their art. Not one of these books can be understood unless we read the two others; but of the three, the only quite trustworthy one is the last. The acts of a nation may be triumphant by its good fortune; and its words mighty by the genius of a few of its children: but its art, only by the general gifts and common sympathies of the race.

Again, the policy of a nation may be compelled, and, therefore, not indicative of its true character. Its words may be false, while yet the race remain unconscious of their falsehood; and no historian can assuredly detect the hypocrisy. But art is always instinctive; and the honesty or pretence of it are therefore open to the day. The Delphic oracle may or may not have been spoken by an honest priestess,—we cannot tell by the words of it; a liar may rationally believe them a lie, such as he would himself have spoken; and a true man, with equal reason, may believe them spoken in truth. But there is no question possible in art: at a glance (when we have learned to read), we know the religion of Angelico to be sincere, and of Titian, assumed.

The evidence, therefore, of the third book is the most vital to our knowledge of any nation's life ; and the history of Venice is chiefly written in such manuscript. It once lay open on the waves, miraculous, like St. Cuthbert's book,—a golden legend on countless leaves : now, like Baruch's roll, it is being cut with the penknife, leaf by leaf, and consumed in the fire of the most brutish of the fiends. What fragments of it may yet be saved in blackened scroll, like those withered Cottonian relics in our National library, of which so much has been redeemed by love and skill, this book will help you, partly, to read. Partly,—for I know only myself in part ; but what I tell you, so far as it reaches, will be truer than you have heard hitherto, because founded on this absolutely faithful witness, despised by other historians, if not wholly unintelligible to them.

I am obliged to write shortly, being too old now to spare time for any thing more than needful work ; and I write at speed, careless of afterwards remediable mistakes, of which adverse readers may gather as many as they choose : that to which such readers are adverse will be found truth that can abide any quantity of adversity.

As I can get my chapters done, they shall be published in this form, for such service as they can presently do.

The entire book will consist of not more than twelve such parts, with two of appendices, forming two volumes : if I can get what I have to say into six parts, with one appendix, all the better.

Two separate little guides, one to the Academy, the other to San Giorgio de' Schiavoni, will, I hope, be ready with the opening numbers of this book, which must depend somewhat on their collateral illustration; and what I find likely to be of service to the traveller in my old 'Stones of Venice' is in course of re-publication, with further illustration of the complete works of Tintoret. But this cannot be ready till the autumn; and what I have said of the mightiest of Venetian masters, in my lecture on his relation to Michael Angelo, will be enough at present to enable the student to complete the range of his knowledge to the close of the story of 'St. Mark's Rest.'

CONTENTS.

CONTENTS.

SUPPLEMENT I.

SUPPLEMENT II.

Edited by J. Ruskin.

APPENDIX TO CHAPTER VIII.

Edited by J. Ruskin.

ST. MARK'S REST.

CHAPTER I.

THE BURDEN OF TYRE.

Go first into the Piazzetta, and stand anywhere in the shade, where you can well see its two granite pillars.

Your Murray tells you that they are 'famous,' and that the one is "surmounted by the bronze lion of St. Mark, the other by the statue of St. Theodore, the Protector of the Republic."

It does not, however, tell you why, or for what the pillars are 'famous.' Nor, in reply to a question which might conceivably occur to the curious, why St. Theodore should protect the Republic by standing on a crocodile : nor whether the "bronze lion of St. Mark" was cast by Sir Edwin Landseer,—or some more ancient and ignorant person ; nor what these rugged corners of limestone rock, at the bases of the granite, were perhaps once in the shape of. Have you any idea why, for the sake of any such things, these pillars were once, or should yet be, more renowned than the Monument, or the column of the Place Vendôme, both of which are much bigger ?

Well, they are famous, first, in memorial of something which is better worth remembering than the fire of London, or the achievements of the great Napoleon. And they are famous, or used to be, among artists, because they are beautiful columns; nay, as far as we old artists know, the most beautiful columns at present extant and erect in the conveniently visitable world.

Each of these causes of their fame I will try in some dim degree to set before you.

I said they were set there in memory of *things*,—not of the man who did the things. They are to Venice, in fact, what the Nelson column would be to London, if, instead of a statue of Nelson and a coil of rope, on the top of it, we had put one of the four Evangelists, and a saint, for the praise of the Gospel and of Holiness :— trusting the memory of Nelson to our own souls.

However, the memory of the Nelson of Venice, being now seven hundred years old, has more or less faded from the heart of Venice herself, and seldom finds its way into the heart of a stranger. Somewhat concerning him, though a stranger, you may care to hear, but you must hear it in quiet; so let your boatman take you across to San Giorgio Maggiore; there you can moor your gondola under the steps in the shade, and read in peace, looking up at the pillars when you like.

In the year 1117, when the Doge Ordeláfo Falier had been killed under the walls of Zara, Venice chose, for his successor, Domenico Michiel, Michael of the Lord, 'Cattolico nomo e audace,' * a catholic and brave man, the servant of God and of St. Michael.

---

* **Marin Sanuto.** Vitæ Ducum Venetorum, henceforward quoted as V., with references to the pages of Muratori's edition. See Appendix, Art. 1, which with following appendices will be given in a separate number as soon as there are enough to form one.

Another of Mr. Murray's*publications for your general assistance ('Sketches from Venetian History') informs you that, at this time, the ambassadors of the King of Jerusalem (the second Baldwin) were "awakening the pious zeal, and stimulating the commercial appetite, of the Venetians."

This elegantly balanced sentence is meant to suggest to you that the Venetians had as little piety as we have ourselves, and were as fond of money—that article being the only one which an Englishman could now think of, as an object of "commercial appetite."

The facts which take this aspect to the lively cockney, are, in reality, that Venice was sincerely pious, and intensely covetous. But not covetous merely of money. She was covetous, first, of fame; secondly, of kingdom; thirdly, of pillars of marble and granite, such as these that you see; lastly, and quite principally, of the relics of good people. Such an 'appetite,' glib-tongued cockney friend, is not wholly 'commercial.'

To the nation in this religiously covetous hunger, Baldwin appealed, a captive to the Saracen. The Pope sent letters to press his suit, and the Doge Michael called the State to council in the church of St. Mark. There he, and the Primate of Venice, and her nobles, and such of the people as had due entrance with them, by way of beginning the business, celebrated the Mass of the Holy Spirit. Then the Primate read the Pope's letters aloud to the assembly; then the Doge made the assembly a speech. And there was no opposition party in that parliament to make opposition speeches; and there were no reports of the speech next morning in any Times or Daily Telegraph. And there were no plenipotentiaries sent to the East, and back again. But the vote passed for war.

The Doge left his son in charge of the State ; and sailed for the Holy Land, with forty galleys and twenty-eight beaked ships of battle—"ships which were painted with divers colors," * far seen in pleasant splendor.

Some faded likeness of them, twenty years ago, might be seen in the painted sails of the fishing boats which lay crowded, in lowly lustre, where the development of civilization now only brings black steam-tugs,† to bear the people of Venice to the bathing-machines of Lido, covering their Ducal Palace with soot, and consuming its sculptures with sulphurous acid.

The beaked ships of the Doge Michael had each a hundred oars,—each oar pulled by two men, not accommodated with sliding seats, but breathed well for their great boat-race between the shores of Greece and Italy,—whose names, alas, with the names of their trainers, are noteless in the journals of the barbarous time.

They beat their way across the waves, nevertheless, ‡ to the place by the sea-beach in Palestine where Dorcas worked for the poor, and St. Peter lodged with his namesake tanner. There, showing first but a squadron of a few ships, they drew the Saracen fleet out to sea, and so set upon them.

---

* 'The Acts of God, by the Franks.' Afterwards quoted as G. (Gesta Dei). Again, see Appendix, Art. 1.

† The sails may still be seen scattered farther east along the Riva ; but the beauty of the scene, which gave some image of the past, was in their combination with the Ducal Palace,—not with the new French and English Restaurants.

‡ Oars, of course, for calm, and adverse winds, only ; bright sails full to the helpful breeze.

And the Doge, in his true Duke's place, first in his beaked ship, led for the Saracen admiral's, struck her, and sunk her. And his host of falcons followed to the slaughter: and to the prey also,—for the battle was not without gratification of the commercial appetite. The Venetians took a number of ships containing precious silks, and " a quantity of drugs and pepper."

After which battle, the Doge went up to Jerusalem, there to take further counsel concerning the use of his Venetian power; and, being received there with honor, kept his Christmas in the mountain of the Lord.

In the council of war that followed, debate became stern whether to undertake the siege of Tyre or Ascalon. The judgments of men being at pause, the matter was given to the judgment of God. They put the names of the two cities in an urn, on the altar of the Church of the Sepulchre. An orphan child was taken to draw the lots, who, putting his hand into the urn, drew out the name of TYRE.

Which name you may have heard before, and read perhaps words concerning her fall—careless always when the fall took place, or whose sword smote her.

She was still a glorious city, still queen of the treasures of the sea ; * chiefly renowned for her work in glass and in purple ; set in command of a rich plain, " irrigated with plentiful and perfect waters, famous for its sugar-canes ; ' fortissima,' she herself, upon her rock, double walled towards the sea, treble walled to the land ; and, to all seeming, inconquerable but by famine."

---

* " Passava tuttavia per la piu popolosa e commerciante di Siria."— Romanin, 'Storia Documentata di Venezia,' Venice, 1853, vol. ii., whence I take what else is said in the text ; but see in the Gesta Dei, the older Marin Sanuto, lib. iii., pars. vi. cap. xii., and pars. xiv. cap. ii.

For their help in this great siege, the Venetians made their conditions.

That in every city subject to the King of Jerusalem, the Venetians should have a street, a square, a bath, and a bakehouse: that is to say, a place to live in, a place to meet in, and due command of water and bread, all free of tax; that they should use their own balances, weights, and measures (not by any means false ones, you will please to observe); and that the King of Jerusalem should pay annually to the Doge of Venice, on the Feast of St. Peter and St. Paul, three hundred Saracen byzants.

Such, with due approval of the two Apostles of the Gentiles, being the claims of these Gentile mariners from the King of the Holy City, the same were accepted in these terms: "In the name of the Holy and undivided Trinity of the Father, the Son, and the Holy Ghost, these are the treaties which Baldwin, second King of the Latins in Jerusalem, made with St. Mark and Dominicus Michaël"; and ratified by the signatures of—

GUARIMOND, Patriarch of Jerusalem;

EBREMAR, Archbishop of Cæsarea;

BERNARD, Archbishop of Nazareth;

ASQUIRIN, Bishop of Bethlehem;

GOLDUMUS, Abbot of St. Mary's, in the Vale of Jehoshaphat;

ACCHARD, Prior of the Temple of the Lord;

GERARD, Prior of the Holy Sepulchre;

ARNARD, Prior of Mount Syon; and

HUGO DE PAGANO, Master of the Soldiers of the Temple. With others many, whose names are in the chronicle of Andrea Dandolo.

And thereupon the French crusaders by land, and the Venetians by sea, drew line of siege round Tyre.

You will not expect me here, at St. George's steps, to give account of the various mischief done on each other with the dart, the stone, and the fire, by the Christian and Saracen, day by day. Both were at last wearied, when report came of help to the Tyrians by an army from Damascus, and a fleet from Egypt. Upon which news, discord arose in the invading camp; and rumor went abroad that the Venetians would desert their allies, and save themselves in their fleet. These reports coming to the ears of the Doge, he took (according to tradition) the sails from his ships' masts, and the rudders from their sterns,* and brought sails, rudders, and tackle ashore, and into the French camp, adding to these, for his pledge, "grave words."

The French knights, in shame of their miscreance, bade him refit his ships. The Count of Tripoli and William of Bari were sent to make head against the Damascenes; and the Doge, leaving ships enough to blockade the port, sailed himself, with what could be spared, to *find* the Egyptian fleet. He sailed to Alexandria, showed his sails along the coast in defiance, and returned.

Meantime his coin for payment of his mariners was spent. He did not care to depend on remittances. He

---

* By doing this he left his fleet helpless before an enemy, for naval warfare at this time depended wholly on the fine steering of the ships at the moment of onset. But for all ordinary manœuvres necessary for the safety of the fleet in harbor, their oars were enough. Andrea Dandolo says he took a plank ("tabula") out of each ship,—a more fatal injury. I suspect the truth to have been that he simply un-shipped the rudders, and brought them into camp; a grave speech-less symbol, earnest enough, but not costly of useless labor.

struck a coinage of leather, with St. Mark's and his own shield on it, promising his soldiers that for every leathern rag, so signed, at Venice, there should be given a golden zecchin. And his word was taken; and his word was kept.

So the steady siege went on, till the Tyrians lost hope, and asked terms of surrender.

They obtained security of person and property, to the indignation of the Christian soldiery, who had expected the sack of Tyre. The city was divided into three parts, of which two were given to the King of Jerusalem, the third to the Venetians.

How Baldwin governed his two thirds, I do not know, nor what capacity there was in the Tyrians of being governed at all. But the Venetians, for their third part, appointed a '*bailo*' to do civil justice, and a '*viscount*' to answer for military defence; and appointed magistrates under these, who, on entering office, took the following oath :—

" I swear on the holy Gospels of God, that sincerely and without fraud I will do right to all men who are under the jurisdiction of Venice in the city of Tyre ; and to every other who shall be brought before me for judgment, according to the ancient use and law of the city. And so far as I know not, and am left uninformed of that, I will act by such rule as shall appear to me just, according to the appeal and answer. Farther, I will give faithful and honest counsel to the Bailo and the Viscount, *when I am asked for it ;* and if they share any secret with me, I will keep it ; neither will I procure by fraud, good to a friend, nor evil to an enemy." And thus the Venetian state planted stable colonies in Asia.

Thus far Romanin; to whom, nevertheless, it does not occur to ask what 'establishing colonies in Asia' meant for Venice. Whether they were in Asia, Africa, or the Island of Atlantis, did not at this time greatly matter; but it mattered infinitely that they were *colonies living in friendly relations with the Saracen*, and that at the very same moment arose cause of quite other than friendly relations, between the Venetian and the Greek.

For while the Doge Michael fought for the Christian king at Jerusalem, the Christian emperor at Byzantium attacked the defenceless states of Venice, on the mainland of Dalmatia, and seized their cities. Whereupon the Doge set sail homewards, fell on the Greek islands of the Egean, and took the spoil of them; seized Cephalonia; recovered the lost cities of Dalmatia; compelled the Greek emperor to sue for peace,—gave it, in angry scorn; and set his sails at last for his own Rialto, with the sceptres of Tyre and of Byzantium to lay at the feet of Venice.

Spoil also he brought, enough, of such commercial kind as Venice valued. These pillars that you look upon, of rosy and gray rock; and the dead bodies of St. Donato and St. Isidore.

He thus returned, in 1126: Fate had left him yet four years to live. In which, among other homely work, he made the beginning for you (oh much civilized friend, you will at least praise him in this) of these mighty gaseous illuminations by which Venice provides for your seeing her shop-wares by night, and provides against your seeing the moon, or stars, or sea.

For, finding the narrow streets of Venice dark, and opportune for robbers, he ordered that at the heads of them there should be set little tabernacles for images of the saints, and before each a light kept burning. Thus he commands,—not as thinking that the saints themselves had need of candles, but that they would gladly grant to poor mortals in danger, material no less than heavenly light.

And having in this pretty and lowly beneficence ended what work he had to do in this world, feeling his strength fading, he laid down sword and ducal robe together ; and became a monk, in this island of St. George, at the shore of which you are reading : but the old monastery on it which sheltered him was destroyed long ago, that this stately Palladian portico might be built, to delight Mr. Eustace on his classical tour,—and other such men of renown,—and persons of excellent taste, like yourself.

And there he died, and was buried ; and there he lies, virtually tombless : the place of his grave you find by going down the steps on your right hand behind the altar, leading into what was yet a monastery before the last Italian revolution, but is now a finally deserted loneliness.

Over his grave there is a heap of frightful modern upholsterer's work,—Longhena's ; his first tomb (of which you may see some probable likeness in those at the side of St. John and St. Paul) being removed as too modest and timeworn for the vulgar Venetian of the seventeenth century ; and this, that you see, put up to please the Lord Mayor and the beadles.

The old inscription was copied on the rotten black slate which is breaking away in thin flakes, dimmed by dusty salt. The beginning of it yet remains : "Here lies the Terror of the Greeks." Read also the last lines :

" Whosoever thou art, who comest to behold this tomb of his, bow thyself down before God, because of him."

' Of these things, then, the two pillars before you are ' famous ' in memorial. What in themselves they possess deserving honor, we will next try to discern. But you must row a little nearer to the pillars, so as to see them clearly.

CHAPTER II.

I said these pillars were the most beautiful known to me ; but you must understand this saying to be of the whole pillar—group of base, shaft, and capital—not only of their shafts.

You know so much of architecture, perhaps, as that an 'order' of it is the system, connecting a shaft with its capital and cornice. And you can surely feel so much of architecture, as thàt, if you took the heads off these pillars, and set the granite shafts simply upright on the pavement, they would perhaps remind you of ninepins, or rolling-pins, but would in no wise contribute either to respectful memory of the Doge Michael, or to the beauty of the Piazzetta.

Their beauty, which has been so long instinctively felt by artists, consists then first in the proportion, and then in the propriety of their several parts. Do not confuse proportion with propriety. An elephant is as properly made as a stag ; but he is not so gracefully proportioned. In fine architecture, and all other fine arts, grace and propriety meet.

I will take the fitness first. You see that both these pillars have wide bases of successive steps. * You can feel that these would be 'improper' round the pillars of

* Restored,—but they always must have had them, in some such proportion.

an arcade in which people walked, because they would be in the way. But they are proper here, because they tell us the pillar is to be isolated, and that it is a monument of importance. Look from these shafts to the arcade of the Ducal Palace. Its pillars have been found fault with for wanting bases. But they were meant to be walked beside without stumbling.

Next, you see the tops of the capitals of the great pillars spread wide, into flat tables. You can feel, surely, that these are entirely 'proper,' to afford room for the statues they are to receive, and that the edges, which bear no weight, may 'properly' extend widely. But suppose a weight of superincumbent wall were to be laid on these pillars? The extent of capital which is now graceful, would then be weak and ridiculous.

Thus far of propriety, whose simple laws are soon satisfied : next, of proportion.

You see that one of the shafts—the St. Theodore's— is much more slender than the other.

One general law of proportion is that a slender shaft should have a slender capital, and a ponderous shaft, a ponderous one.

But had this law been here followed, the companion pillars would have instantly become ill-matched. The eye would have discerned in a moment the fat pillar and the lean. They would never have become the fraternal pillars—'the two' of the Piazzetta.

With subtle, scarcely at first traceable, care, the designer varied the curves and weight of his capitals ; and gave the massive head to the slender shaft, and the slender capital to the massive shaft. And thus they stand in symmetry, and uncontending equity.

Next, for the form of these capitals themselves, and the date of them.

You will find in the guide-books that though the shafts were brought home by the Doge in 1126, no one could be found able to set them up, until the year 1171, when a certain Lombard, called Nicholas of the Barterers, raised them, and for reward of such engineering skill, bargained that he might keep tables for forbidden games of chance between the shafts. Whereupon the Senate ordered that executions should also take place between them.

You read, and smile, and pass on with a dim sense of having heard something like a good story.

Yes; of which I will pray you to remark, that at that uncivilized time, games of chance were forbidden in Venice, and that in these modern civilized times they are not forbidden; and one, that of the lottery, even promoted by the Government as gainful: and that perhaps the Venetian people might find itself more prosperous on the whole by obeying that law of their fathers, * and ordering that no lottery should be drawn, except in a place where somebody had been hanged. † But the curious thing is that while this pretty story is never forgotten, about the raising of the pillars, nothing is ever so much as questioned about who put their tops and bases to them! —nothing about the resolution that lion or saint should stand to preach on them,—nothing about the Saint's ser-

* Have you ever read the ' Fortunes of Nigel ' with attention to the moral of it ?

† It orders now that the drawing should be at the foot of St. Mark's Campanile ; and, weekly, the mob of Venice, gathered for the event, fills the marble porches with its anxious murmur.

mon, or the Lion's; nor enough, even, concerning the
name or occupation of Nicholas the Barterer, to lead the
pensive traveller into a profitable observance of the appointment of Fate, that in this Tyre of the West, the city
of merchants, her monuments of triumph over the Tyre of
the East should forever stand signed by a tradition re-
cording the stern judgment of her youth against the gam-
bler's lust, which was the passion of her old age.

But now of the capitals themselves. If you are the
least interested in architecture, should it not be of some
importance to you to note the style of them? Twelfth
century capitals, as fresh as when they came from the
chisel, are not to be seen every day, or everywhere—
much less capitals like these, a fathom or so broad and
high! And if you know the architecture of England and
France in the twelfth century, you will find these capitals
still more interesting from their extreme difference in
manner. Not the least like our clumps and humps and
cushions, are they? For these are living Greek work,
still; not savage Norman or clumsy Northumbrian, these;
but of pure Corinthian race; yet, with Venetian practical-
ness of mind, solidified from the rich clusters of light leafage which were their ancient form. You must find time
for a little practical cutting of capitals yourself, before
you will discern the beauty of these. There is nothing
like a little work with the fingers for teaching the eyes.

As you go home to lunch, therefore, buy a pound of
Gruyère cheese, or of any other equally tough and bad,
with as few holes in it as may be. And out of this
pound of cheese, at lunch, cut a solid cube as neatly as
you can.

Now all treatment of capitals depends primarily on the

way in which a cube of stone, like this of cheese, is left
by the carver square at the top, to carry the wall, and cut
round at the bottom to fit its circular pillar. Proceed
therefore to cut your cube so that it may fit a round pillar
of cheese at the bottom, such as is extracted, for tasting,
by magnanimous cheesemongers, for customers worth their
while. Your first natural proceeding will of course be to
cut off four corners; so making an octagon at the bottom,
which is a good part of the way to a circle. Now if you
cut off those corners with rather a long, sweeping cut, as
if you were cutting a pencil, you will see that already you
have got very near the shape of the Piazzetta capitals.
But you will come still nearer, if you make each of these
simple corner-cuts into two narrower ones, thus bringing
the lower portion of your bit of cheese into a twelve-sided
figure. And you will see that each of these double-cut
angles now has taken more or less the shape of a leaf,
with its central rib at the angle. And if, further, with
such sculpturesque and graphic talent as may be in you,
you scratch out the real shape of a leaf at the edge of the
cuts and run furrows from its outer lobes to the middle,—
behold, you have your Piazzetta capital. *All but* have it,
I should say; only this 'all but' is nearly all the good of
it, which comes of the exceeding fineness with which the
simple curves are drawn, and reconciled.

Nevertheless, you will have learned, if sagacious in such
matters, by this quarter of an hour's carving, so much of
architectural art as will enable you to discern, and to enjoy the treatment of, all the twelfth and thirteenth century capitals in Venice, which, without exception, when
of native cutting, are concave bells like this, with either a
springing leaf, or a bending boss of stone which would be-

come a leaf if it were furrowed, at the **angles**. But the fourteenth century brings a change.

Before I tell you what took place in the fourteenth century, you must cut yourself another cube of Gruyère cheese. You see that in the one you have made a capital of already, a good weight of cheese out of the cube has been cut away in tapering down those long-leaf corners. Suppose you try now to make a capital of it without cutting away so much cheese. If you begin half way down the side, with a shorter but more curved **cut, you** may reduce the base to the same form, and—supposing you are working in **marble instead** of cheese—you have not only much less trouble, **but you keep a** much more solid block of stone to bear superincumbent weight.

Now you may go back to the Piazzetta, and, thence proceeding, so as to get well in front of the Ducal Palace, look first to the Greek shaft capitals, and then to those **of** the Ducal Palace upper arcade. **You** will recognize, especially in those nearest the Ponte della Paglia (at least, if you have an eye in your head), the shape of your second block of Gruyère,—decorated, it is true, in manifold ways, but essentially shaped like your most cheaply cut block of cheese. Modern architects, in imitating these capitals, can reach as far as—imitating your Gruyère. Not being able to decorate the block when they have got it, they declare that decoration is "a superficial merit."

Yes,—very superficial. Eyelashes and eyebrows—lips and nostrils—chin-dimples and curling hair, are all very superficial things, wherewith Heaven decorates the human skull; making the **maid's** face of it, or the knight's. Nevertheless, what I want you to notice now, is but the form of the block of **Istrian** stone, usually with a spiral,

more or less elaborate, on each of its projecting angles.
For there is infinitude of history in that solid angle, prevailing over the light Greek leaf. That *is* related to our
humps and clumps at Durham and Winchester. Here is,
indeed, Norman temper, prevailing over Byzantine; and
it means,—the outcome of that quarrel of Michiel with
the Greek Emperor. It means—western for eastern life,
in the mind of Venice. It means her fellowship with the
western chivalry; her triumph in the Crusades,—triumph
over her own foster nurse, Byzantium.

Which significances of it, and many others with them,
if we would follow, we must leave our stone-cutting for a
little while, and map out the chart of Venetian history
from its beginning into such masses as we may remember
without confusion. .

But, since this will take time, and we cannot quite tell
how long it may be before we get back to the twelfth
century again, and to our Piazzetta shafts, let me complete
what I can tell you of these at once.

In the first place, the Lion of St. Mark is a splendid
piece of eleventh or twelfth century bronze. I know that
by the style of him; but have never found out where he
came from.* I may now chance on it, however, at any
moment in other quests. Eleventh or twelfth century,
the Lion—fifteenth, or later, his wings; very delicate in
feather-workmanship, but with little lift or strike in them;

* "He"—the actual piece of forged metal, I mean. (See Appendix
II. for account of its recent botchings.) Your modern English ex-
plainers of him have never heard, I observe, of any such person as an
'Evangelist,' or of any Christian symbol of such a being! See page
42 of Mr. Adams' 'Venice Past and Present' (Edinburgh and New
York, 1852).

decorative mainly. Without doubt his first wings were
thin sheets of beaten bronze, shred into plumage ; far
wider in their sweep than these.†

The statue of St. Theodore, whatever its age, is wholly
without merit. I can't make it out myself, nor find
record of it : in a stonemason's yard, I should have passed
it as modern. But this merit of the statue is here of little
consequence,—the power of it being wholly in its meaning.

St. Theodore represents the power of the Spirit of God
in all noble and useful animal life, conquering what is
venomous, useless, or in decay : he differs from St. George
in contending with material evil, instead of with sinful
passion : the crocodile on which he stands is the Dragon
of Egypt ; slime-begotten of old, worshipped in its malignant power, for a God. St. Theodore's martyrdom was
for breaking such idols ; and with beautiful instinct Venice took him in her earliest days for her protector and
standard-bearer, representing the heavenly life of Christ
in men, prevailing over chaos and the deep.

With far more than instinct,—with solemn recognition,
and prayerful vow, she took him in the pride of her
chivalry, in mid-thirteenth century, for the master of that
chivalry in their gentleness of home ministries. The
‘ Mariegola ’ (Mother-Law) of the school of St. Theodore,
by kind fate yet preserved to us, contains the legend they
believed, in its completeness, and their vow of service and
companionship in all its terms.

---

† I am a little proud of this guess, for before correcting this sentence in type, I found the sharp old wings represented faithfully in
the woodcut of Venice in 1480, in the Correr Museum. Durer, in
1500, draws the present wings ; so that we get their date fixed within
twenty years.

Either of which, if you care to understand,—several other matters and writings must be understood first ; and, among others, a pretty piece of our own much boasted,— how little obeyed,—Mother-Law, sung still by statute in our churches at least once in the month ; the eighty-sixth Psalm. "Her foundations are in the holy Mountains." I hope you can go on with it by heart, or at least have your Bible in your portmanteau. In the remote possibility that you may have thought its carriage unnecessarily expensive, here is the Latin psalm, with its modern Italian-Catholic * translation ; watery enough, this last, but a clear and wholesome, though little vapid, dilution and diffusion of its text,—making much intelligible to the Protestant reader, which his ' private judgment ' might occasionally have been at fault in.

Fundamenta eius in montibus sanctis : diligit Dominus portas Sion super omnia tabernacula Iacob.

Gloriosa dicta sunt de te, civitas Dei.

Memor ero Rahab et Babylonis, scientium me.

Ecce alienigenae, et Tyrus, et populus Æthiopum hi fuerunt illic.

Gerusalemme è fabbricata sopra i santi monti : Iddio ne prende più cura, e l' ama più che tutti gli altri luoghi che dal suo popolo sono abitati.

Quante cose tutte piene di lode sono state dette di voi, città di Dio !

Non lascerò nell' oblivione nè l' Egitto nè Babilonia, dacchè que' popoli mi avranno riconosciuto per loro Dio.

Quanti popoli stranieri, Tiri, Etiopi, sino a quel punto miei nemici, verranno a prestarmi i loro omaggi.

* From the ' Uffizio della B. V. Maria, Italiano o Latino, per tutti i tempi dell' anno, del Padre G. Croiset,' a well printed and most serviceable little duodecimo volume, for any one wishing to know somewhat of Roman Catholic offices. Published in Milan and Venice.

Nunquid Sion dicet : Homo et homo natus est in ea, et ipse fundavit eam Altissimus ?	Ognuno dirà allora : Vedete come questa città si è popolata ! l' Altissimo l' ha fondata e vuole metterla in fiore.
Dominus narrabit in scripturis populorum et principum : horum qui fuerunt in ea.	Egli perciò è l' unico che conosca il numero del popolo e de' grandi che ne sono gli abitanti.
Sicut lætantium omnium habitatio est in te.	Non vi è vera felicità, se non per coloro che vi hanne l' abitazione.

Reading then the psalm in these words, you have it as the Western Christians sang it ever since St. Jerome wrote it into such interpretation for them ; and you must try to *feel* it as these Western Christians of Venice felt it, having now their own street in the holy city, and their covenant with the Prior of Mount Syon, and of the Temple of the Lord : they themselves having struck down Tyre with their own swords, taken to themselves her power, and now reading, as of themselves, the encompassing benediction of the prophecy for all Gentile nations, "Ecce alienigenæ—et Tyrus." A notable piece of Scripture for them, to be dwelt on, in every word of it, with all humility of faith.

What then *is* the meaning of the two verses just preceding these ?—

" Glorious things are spoken of thee, thou City of God. I will make mention of Rahab and Babylon, with them that know me."

If you like to see a curious mistake at least of *one* Protestant's ' private judgment' of this verse, you must look at my reference to it in Fors Clavigera of April, 1876, p. 110, with its correction by Mr. Gordon, in Fors for June, 1876, pp. 178–203, all containing variously useful notes on these verses; of which the gist is, however, that the 'Rahab' of the Latin text is the Egyptian 'Dragon,' the crocodile, signifying in myth, which has now been three thousand years continuous in human mind, the total power of the crocodile-god of Egypt, couchant on his slime, born of it, mistakable for it,—his gray length of unintelligible scales, fissured and wrinkled like dry clay, itself but, as it were, a shelf or shoal of coagulated, malignant earth. He and his company, the deities born of the earth—beast headed,—with only animal cries for voices :—

"Omnigenumque Deûm monstra, et latrator Anubis
  Contra Neptunum et Venerem, contraque Minervam."

This is St. Theodore's Dragon-enemy—Egypt, and her captivity; bondage of the earth, literally to the Israelite, in making bricks of it, the first condition of form for the God : in sterner than mere literal truth, the captivity of the spirit of man, whether to earth or to its creatures.

And St. Theodore's victory is making the earth his pedestal, instead of his adversary; he is the power of gentle and rational life, reigning over the wild creatures and senseless forces of the world. The Latrator Anubis—most senseless and cruel of the guardians of hell—becoming, by human mercy, the faithfullest of creature-friends to man.

Do you think all this work useless in your Venetian guide ? There is not a picture,—not a legend,—scarcely a column or an ornament, in the art of Venice or of Italy, which, by this piece of work, well done, will not become more precious to you. Have you ever, for instance, noticed

how the baying of Cerberus is stopped, in the sixth canto
of Dante,—

> " Il duca mio
> **Prese** *la terra ;* et con piene le pugne
> **La** gitto dentro alle bramose canne."

(To the *three*, therefore plural.) It is one of the innumerable subtleties which mark Dante's perfect knowledge
—inconceivable except as a form of inspiration—of the
inner meaning of every myth, whether of classic or Christian theology, known in his day.

Of the relation of the dog, horse, and eagle to the chivalry of Europe, you will find, if you care to read, more
noted, in relation to part of the legend of St. Theodore,
in the Fors of March, this year; the rest of his legend.
with what is notablest in his ' Mariegola,' I will tell you
when we come to examine Carpaccio's canonized birds and
beasts; of which, to refresh you after this piece of hard
ecclesiastical reading (for I can't tell you about the bases
of the pillars to-day. We must get into another humor to
see these), you may see within five minutes' walk, three
together, in the little chapel of St. George of the Schiavoni: St. George's ' Porphyrio,' the bird of chastity, with
the bent spray of sacred vervain in its beak, at the foot of
the steps on which St. George is baptizing the princess;
St. Jerome's lion, being introduced to the monastery (with
resultant effect on the minds of the brethren); and St.
Jerome's dog, watching his master translating the Bible,
with highest complacency of approval.

And of St. Theodore himself you may be glad to know
that he was a very historical and substantial saint as late
as the fifteenth century, for in the Inventory of the goods
and chattels of his scuola, made by order of its master

(Gastoldo), and the companions, in the year 1450, the first
article is the body of St. Theodore, with the bed it lies on,
covered by a coverlid of "paño di grano di seta, brocado
de oro fino." So late as the middle of the fifteenth century (certified by the inventario fatto a di XXX. de
Novembrio MCCCCL. per. Sr nanni di piero de la
colōna, Gastoldo, e snoi campagni, de tutte reliquie e
arnesi e beni, se trova in questa hora presente in la nostra
scuola), here lay this treasure, dear to the commercial
heart of Venice.

Oh, good reader, who hast ceased to count the Dead
bones of men for thy treasure, hast thou then thy Dead
laid up in the hands of the Living God?

CHAPTER III.

TWICE one is two, and twice two is four; but twice one is not three, and twice two is not six, whatever Shylock may wish, or say, in the matter. In wholesome memory of which arithmetical, and (probably) eternal, fact, and in loyal defiance of Shylock and his knife, I write down for you these figures, large and plain:

1.   2.   4.

Also in this swiftly progressive ratio, the figures may express what modern philosophy considers the rate of progress of Venice, from her days of religion, and golden ducats, to her days of infidelity, and paper notes.

Read them backwards, then, sublime modern philosopher; and they will give you the date of the birth of that foolish Venice of old time, on her narrow island.

4.   2.   1.

In that year, and on the very day—(little foolish Venice used to say, when she was a very child),—in which, once upon a time, the world was made; and, once upon another time—the Ave Maria first said,—the first stone of Venice was laid on the sea sand, in the name of St. James the fisher.

I think you had better go and see with your own eyes.—tread with your own foot,—the spot of her nativity: so

much of a spring day as the task will take, cannot often
be more profitably spent, nor more affectionately towards
God and man, if indeed you love either of them.

So, from the Grand Hotel,—or the Swiss Pension—or
the duplicate Danieli with the drawbridge,—or wherever
else among the palaces of resuscitated Venice you abide,
congratulatory modern ambassador to the Venetian Senate,—please, to-day, walk through the Merceria, and
through the Square of St. Bartholomew, where is the little
octagon turret-chapel in the centre, for sale of news: and
cross the Rialto—not in the middle of it, but on the right
hand side, crossing from St. Mark's. You will probably
find it very dirty,—it may be, indecently dirty,—that is
modern progress, and Mr. Buckle's civilization; rejoice in
it with a thankful heart, and stay in it placidly, after crossing the height of the bridge, when you come down just on
a level with the capitals of the first story of the black and
white, all but ruined, Palace of the Camerlenghi; Treasurers of Venice, built for them when she began to feel
anxious about her accounts. 'Black and white,' I call it,
because the dark lichens of age are yet on its marble—or,
at least, were, in the winter of '76–'77; it may be, even
before these pages get printed, it will be scraped and re-
gilt—or pulled down, to make a railroad station at the
Rialto.

Here standing, if with good eyes, or a good opera glass,
you look back, up to the highest story of the blank and
ugly building on the side of the canal you have just crossed
from,—you will see between two of its higher windows,
the remains of a fresco of a female figure. It is, so far as
I know, the last vestige of the noble fresco painting of
Venice on her outside walls;—Giorgione's,—no less,—

when Titian and he were house-painters,—the Sea-Queen so ranking them, for her pomp, in her proud days. Of this, and of the black and white palace, we will talk another day. I only asked you to look at the fresco just now, because therein is seen the end of *my* Venice,—the Venice I have to tell you of. Yours, of the Grand Hotels and the Peninsular steamers, you may write the history of, for yourself.

Therein,—as it fades away—ends the Venice of St. Mark's Rest. But where she was born, you may now go quite down the steps to see. Down, and through among the fruit-stalls into the little square on the right; then turning back, the low portico is in front of you—not of the ancient church indeed, but of a fifteenth century one —variously translated, in succeeding times, into such small picturesqueness of stage effect as it yet possesses; escaping, by God's grace, however, the fire which destroyed all the other buildings of ancient Venice, round her Rialto square, in 1513.*

Some hundred or hundred and fifty years before that, Venice had begun to suspect the bodies of saints to be a poor property; carrion, in fact,—and not even exchangeable carrion. Living flesh might be bought instead,—perhaps of prettier aspect. So, as I said, for a hundred years or so, she had brought home no relics,—but set her mind on trade-profits, and other practical matters; tending to the achievement of wealth, and its comforts, and dignities. The curious result being, that at that particular moment, when the fire devoured her merchants' square, centre of the

* **Many** chronicles speak of it as burned; but the authoritative inscription of 1601 speaks of it as 'consumed by age,' and is therefore conclusive on this point.

then mercantile world—she happened to have no money in her pocket to build it again with!

Nor were any of her old methods of business again to be resorted to. Her soldiers were now foreign mercenaries, and had to be paid before they would fight; and prayers, she had found out long before our English wiseacre apothecaries' apprentices, were of no use to get either money, or new houses with, at a pinch like this. And there was really nothing for it but doing the thing cheap,—since it had to be done. Fra Giocondo of Verona offered her a fair design; but the city could not afford it. Had to take Scarpagnino's make-shift instead; and with his help, and Sansovino's, between 1520 and 1550, she just managed to botch up—what you see surround the square, of architectural stateliness for her mercantile home. Discovery of the Cape of Good Hope, the main cause of these sorrowful circumstances of hers,—observe sagacious historians.

At all events, I have no doubt the walls were painted red, with some medallions, or other cheap decoration, under the cornices, enough to make the little square look comfortable. Whitewashed and squalid now—it may be left, for this time, without more note of it, as we turn to the little church.*

Your Murray tells you it was built "in its present form" in 1194, and "rebuilt in 1531, but precisely in the old form," and that it "has a fine brick campanile." The fine brick campanile, visible, if you look behind you, on

---

* Do not, if you will trust me, at this time let your guide take you to look at the Gobbo di Rialto, or otherwise interfere with your immediate business.

the other side of the street, belongs to the church of St.
John Elemosinario. And the statement that the church
was "rebuilt in precisely the old form" must also be received with allowances. For the "campanile" here, is in
the most orthodox English Jacobite style of the seventeenth
century, the portico is Venetian fifteenth, the walls are
in no style at all, and the little Madonna inserted in
the middle of them is an exquisitely finished piece of the
finest work of 1320 to 1350.

And, alas, the church is not only quite other in form,
but even other in *place*, than it was in the fifth century,
having been moved like a bale of goods, and with apparently as little difficulty as scruple, in 1322, on a report
of the Salt Commissioners about the crowding of shops
round it. And, in sum, of particulars of authentically
certified vicissitudes, the little church has gone through
these following—how many more than these, one cannot
say—but these at least (see Appendix III.):

I. Founded traditionally in 421 (serious doubts whether
on Friday or Saturday, involving others about the year
itself). The tradition is all we need care for.

II. Rebuilt, and adorned with Greek mosaic work by
the Doge Domenico Selvo, in 1073; the Doge having
married a Greek wife, and liking pretty things. Of this
husband and wife you shall hear more, anon.

III. Retouched, and made bright again, getting also
its due share of the spoil of Byzantium sent home by
Henry Dandolo, 1174.

IV. Dressed up again, and moved out of the buyers'
and sellers' way, in 1322.

V. 'Instaurated' into a more splendid church (dicto
templo in splendidiorem ecclesiam instaurato) by the

elected plebanus, **Natalis Regia, desirous of** having the church devoted to *his* honor instead of St. James's, 1531.

VI. Lifted up (and most likely therefore first much pulled down), to keep the water from coming into it, in 1601, when the double arched campanile was built, and the thing finally patched **together** in the present form. Doubtless, soon, by farther '·progresso' to become a provision, or, perhaps, a petroleum-store, Venice having no more need of temples ; and being, as far as I can observe, ashamed of having so many, overshadowing her buyers and sellers. Better rend the veils in twain forever, if convenient storeshops may be formed inside.

These, then, being authentic epochs of change, you may decipher at ease the writing of each of them,—what is left of it. The campanile with the ugly head in the centre of it is your final Art result, 1601. The portico in front of you is Natalis **Regia's** 'instauration' of the church as it stood after 1322, retaining the wooden simplicities of bracket above the pillars of the early loggia ; the Madonna, as I said, is a piece of the 1320 to 1350 work ; and of earlier is no vestige here. But if you will walk twenty **steps round** the church, at the back of it, on the low gable, **you will** see an inscription in firmly graven long Roman letters, under a cross, similarly inscribed.

That **is** a vestige of the eleventh century church ; nay, more than vestige, the *Voice* of it—Sibylline,—left when its body had died.'

Which **I will** ask you to hear, in a little while. But first you shall see also a few of the true stones of the older **Temple. Enter it now** ; and reverently ; for though at first, amidst wretched whitewash and stucco, you will scarcely see the true marble, those six pillars

and their capitals are yet actual remnants and material
marble of the venerable church; probably once extend-
ing into more arches in the nave; but this transept ceiling of wagon vault, with the pillars that carry it, is true
remnant of a mediaeval church, and, in all likelihood, true
image of the earliest of all—of the first standard of
Venice, planted, under which to abide; the Cross, en-
graven on the sands thus in relief, with two little pieces
of Roman vaulting, set cross wise;—your modern engi-
neers will soon make as large, in portable brickwork, for
London drains, admirable, worshipful, for the salvation of
London mankind:—here artlessly rounded, and with
small cupola above the crossing.

Thus she set her sign upon the shore; some knot of
gelatinous seaweed there checking the current of the
'Deep Stream,' which sweeps round, as you see, in that
sigma of canal, as the Wharfe round the shingly bank of
Bolton Abbey,—a notablest Crook of Lune, this; and
Castrum, here, on sands that will abide.

It is strange how seldom rivers have been named from
their depth. Mostly they take at once some dear, com-
panionable name, and become gods, or at least living
creatures, to their refreshed people; if not thus Pagan-
named, they are noted by their color, or their purity,—
White River, Black River, Rio Verde, Aqua Dolce,
Fiume di Latte; but scarcely ever, 'Deep River.'

And this Venetian slow-pacing water, not so much as
a river, or any thing like one; but a rivulet, 'fiumicello,'
only, rising in those low mounds of volcanic hill to the
west. " 'Rialto,' 'Rialtum,' '*Pr*ealtum'" (another idea
getting confused with the first), " dal fiumicello di egual
nome che, scendendo dei colli Euganei gettavasi nel

Brenta, con esso scorrendo lungo quelle isole dette appunto Realtine." * 　The serpentine depth, consistent always among consistent shallow, being here vital; and the conception of it partly mingled with that of the power of the open sea—the infinite 'Altum;' sought by the sacred water, as in the dream of Eneas, "lacu fluvius se condidit alto." 　Hence the united word takes, in declining Latin, the shorter form, Rialtum,—properly, in the scholarship of the State-documents, 'Rivoaltus.' 　So also, throughout Venice, the Latin Rivus softens into Rio ; the Latin Ripa into Riva, in the time when you had the running water—not 'canals,' but running brooks of sea,—'lympha fugax,'—trembling in eddies, between, not quays, but banks of pasture land; soft 'campi,' of which, in St. Margaret's field, I have but this autumn seen the last worn vestige trodden away ; and yesterday, Feb. 26th, in the morning, a little tree that was pleasant to me taken up from before the door, because it had heaved the pavement an inch or two out of square; also beside the Academy, a little overhanging momentary shade of boughs hewn away, 'to make the street "bello,"' said the axe-bearer. 　'What,' I asked, 'will it be prettier in summer without its trees?' 　'Non x'e bello il verde,' he answered.† 　True oracle, though he knew not what

---

* Romanin.

† I observe the good people of Edinburgh have the same taste ; and rejoice proudly at having got an asphalt esplanade at the end of Prince's Street, instead of cabbage-sellers. 　Alas ! my Scottish friends ; all that Prince's Street of yours has not so much beauty in it as a single cabbage-stalk, if you had eyes in your heads,—rather the extreme reverse of beauty ; and there is not one of the lassies who now stagger up and down the burning marle in high-heeled boots and French bonnets, who would not look a thousand-fold prettier, and

he said; voice of the modern Church of Venice ranking herself under the black standard of the pit.

I said you should hear the oracle of her ancient
Church in a little while; but you must know why, and
to whom it was spoken, first,—and we must leave the
Rialto for to-day. Look, as you recross its bridge, west-
ward, along the broad-flowing stream; and come here
also, this evening, if the day˒sets calm, for then the
waves of it from the Rialto island to the Cà Foscari, glow
like an Eastern tapestry in soft-flowing crimson, fretted
with gold; and beside them, amidst the tumult of squalid
ruin, remember the words that are the 'burden of
Venice,' as of Tyre :—

" Be still, ye inhabitants of the Isle. Thou whom the
merchants of Zidon, that pass over the sea, have re-
plenished. By great waters, the seed of Sihor, the
harvest of the river, is her revenue; and she is a mart of
nations."

feel, there's no counting how much nobler, bare-headed but for the
snood, and bare-foot on old-fashioned grass by the Nor' loch side,
bringing home from market, basket on arm, pease for papa's dinner,
and a bunch of cherries for baby.

CHAPTER IV.

ST. THEODORE THE CHAIR-SELLER.

THE history of Venice divides itself, with more sharpness than any other I have read, into periods of distinct tendency and character; marked, in their transition, by phenomena no less definite than those of the putting forth the leaves, or setting of the fruit, in a plant;—and as definitely connected by one vitally progressive organization, of which the energy must be studied in its constancy, while its results are classed in grouped system.

If we rightly trace the order, and estimate the duration, of such periods, we understand the life, whether of an organized being or a state. But not to know the time when the seed is ripe, or the soul mature, is to misunderstand the total creature.

In the history of great multitudes, these changes of their spirit, and regenerations (for they are nothing less) of their physical power, take place through so subtle gradations of declining and dawning thought, that the effort to distinguish them seems arbitrary, like separating the belts of a rainbow's color by firmly drawn lines. But, at Venice, the lines are drawn for us by her own hand; and the changes in her temper are indicated by parallel modifications of her policy and constitution, to which historians have always attributed, as to efficient causes, the national fortunes of which they are only the signs and limitation.

In this history, the reader will find little importance attached to these external phenomena of political constitution ; except as labels, or, it may be, securing seals, of the state of the nation's heart. They are merely shapes of amphora, artful and decorative indeed ; tempting to criticism or copy of their form, usefully recordant of different ages of the wine, and having occasionally, by the porousness or perfectness of their clay, effect also on its quality. But it is the grape-juice itself, and the changes in *it*, not in the forms of flask, that we have in reality to study.

Fortunately also, the dates of the great changes are easily remembered ; they fall with felicitous precision at the beginning of centuries, and divide the story of the city, as the pillars of her Byzantine courts, the walls of it, with symmetric stability.

She shall also tell you, as I promised, her own story, in her own handwriting, all through. Not a word shall *I* have to say in the matter ; or aught to do, except to deepen the letters for you when they are indistinct, and sometimes to hold a blank space of her chart of life to the fire of your heart for a little while, until words, written secretly upon it, are seen ;—if, at least, there is fire enough in your own heart to heat them.

And first, therefore, I must try what power of reading you have, when the letters are quite clear. We will take to-day, so please you, the same walk we did yesterday ; but looking at other things, and reading a wider lesson.

As early as you can (in fact, to get the good of this walk, you must be up with the sun), any bright morning, when the streets are quiet, come with me to the front of St. Mark's, to begin our lesson there.

You see that between the arches of its vaults, there are six oblong panels of bas-relief.

Two of these are the earliest pieces of real Venetian work I know of, to show you; but before beginning with them, you must see a piece done by her Greek masters.

Go round therefore to the side farthest from the sea, where, in the first broad arch, you will see a panel of like shape, set horizontally; the sculpture of which represents twelve sheep, six on one side, six on the other, of a throne: on which throne is set a cross; and on the top of the cross a circle; and in the circle, a little caprioling creature.

And outside of all, are two palm trees, one on each side; and under each palm tree, two baskets of dates; and over the twelve sheep, is written in delicate Greek letters "The holy Apostles;" and over the little caprioling creature, "The Lamb."

Take your glass and study the carving of this bas-relief intently. It is full of sweet care, subtlety, tenderness of touch, and mind; and fine cadence and change of line in the little bowing heads and bending leaves. Decorative in the extreme; a kind of stone-stitching, or sampler-work, done with the innocence of a girl's heart, and in a like unlearned fulness. Here is a Christian man, bringing order and loveliness into the mere furrows of stone. Not by any means as learned as a butcher, in the joints of lambs; nor as a grocer, in baskets of dates; nor as a gardener, in endogenous plants: but an artist to the heart's core; and no less true a lover of Christ and His word. Helpless, with his childish art, to carve Christ, he carves a cross, and caprioling little thing in a ring at the top of it. You may try—you—to carve Christ, if you can. Helpless to conceive the Twelve Apostles, these nevertheless are sacred letters for the bearers of the Gospel of Peace.

Of such men **Venice** learned to **touch the** stone;—to become a Lapicida, and furrower **of the marble as** well as the sea.

Now let us go back to that panel on **the** left'side of the central arch in front.*

This, you see, is no more a symbolical **sculpture, but** quite distinctly pictorial, and laboriously ardent to ex-press, though in **very** low relief, a curly-haired personage, handsome, and something like George the Fourth, dressed in richest Roman armor, and sitting in an absurd manner, more or less tailor-fashion, if not cross-legged himself, at least on a conspicuously cross-legged piece of splendid furniture; which, after deciphering the Chinese, or engineer's isometrical, perspective **of** it, you may perceive to be only a gorgeous pic-nic or drawing-stool, apparently **of** portable character, such as are bought (more for **luxury** than labor,—for **the real** working apparatus **is your** tripod) at Messrs. Newman's, or Winsor and Newton's.

Apparently portable, **I say;** by no means intended **as**

---

* Generally **note, when I** say 'right' or 'left' side **of** a church or chapel, **I** mean, either as you enter, or as you look to the altar. It is not safe to say 'north and south,' for Italian churches stand all round the compass; and besides, the phrase would be false of lateral chapels. Transepts are awkward, because often they have an altar instead of an entrance at their ends; it will be least confusing to treat them always **as** large lateral chapels, **and place** them in the series of such chapels at the sides of the nave, calling the sides right and left **as** you look either from the nave into the chapels, or from the nave's centre to the rose window, or other termination of **transept.**

such by the sculptor. Intended for a most permanent and magnificent throne of state; nothing less than a derived form of that Greek **Thronos**, in which you have seen set the cross of the Lamb. Yes; and of the Tyrian and Judæan Thronos—Solomon's, which it frightened the queen of Sheba to see him sitting on. Yes; and of the Egyptian throne of eternal granite, on which colossal Memnon sits, melodious to morning light,—son of Aurora. Yes; and of the throne of Isis-Madonna, and, mightier yet than she, as we return towards the nativity of queens and kings. We must keep at present to our own poor little modern, practical saint—sitting on his portable throne (as at the side of the opera when extra people are let in who shouldn't be); only seven hundred years old. To this cross-legged apparatus the Egyptian throne had dwindled down; it looks even as if the saint who sits on it might begin to think about getting up some day or other.

All the more when you know who he is. Can you read the letters of his name, written beside him?—

    ' SC̄S   GEORGIVS

—Mr. Emerson's purveyor of bacon, no less!* And he *does* look like getting up, when you observe him farther. Unsheathing his sword, is not he?

No; sheathing it. That was the difficult thing he had first to do, as you will find on reading the true legend of him, which *this* sculptor thoroughly knew; in whose conception of the saint one perceives the date of said sculp-

---

* See Fors Clavigera of February, 1873, containing the legend of St. George. This, with the other numbers of Fors referred to in the text of ' St. Mark's Rest,' may be bought at Venice, together with it.

tor, no less than in the stiff work, so dimly yet perceptive of
the ordinary laws of the aspect of things. From the bas-
reliefs of the Parthenon—through sixteen hundred years
of effort, and speech-making, and fighting—human intel-
ligence in the Arts has arrived, here in Venice, thus far.
But having got so far, we shall come to something fresh
soon ! We have become distinctly representative again,
you see ; desiring to show, not a mere symbol of a living
man, but the man himself, as truly as the poor stone-
cutter can carve him. **All** bonds of tyrannous tradition
broken ;—the legend kept, in faith yet ; but the symbol
become natural ; a real **armed** knight, the best he could
form a notion **of ; curly-haired** and handsome ; and, his
also the boast of Dogberry, every thing handsome about
him. Thus far has Venice got in her art schools of the
early thirteenth century. I can date this sculpture to
that time, pretty closely ; earlier, it may be,—not later ;
see afterwards the notes closing this chapter.

And now, if **you so please, we** will **walk** under **the**
clock-tower, and down the **Merceria,** as straight as we can
go. There is **a little crook to the right,** bringing us opposite St. Julian's church **(which,** please, don't stop to
look at just now) ; then, sharply, to the left again, and we
come to the Ponte de' Baratteri,—" Rogue's Bridge"—on
which, as especially a grateful bridge to English business-
feelings, let us reverently pause. It has been widened
lately, you observe,—the use of such bridge being greatly
increased in these times ; and in a convenient angle, out
of passenger current (may you find such wayside with-
drawal in true life), you may stop to look back at the house
immediately above the bridge.

In the wall of which you will see a horizontal panel of

bas-relief, with two shields on each side, bearing six fleur-de-lys. **And this you need not,** I suppose, look for letters on, to **tell** you its subject. Here **is St. George** indeed!—our own beloved **old** sign of the George and Dragon, all correct; and, if **you know your** Seven champions, Sabra too, on the rock, thrilled witness of the fight. **And** see what a dainty St. George, too! Here is no mere tailor's enthronement. Eques, ipso melior Bellerophonti,—how he sits!—how he holds his lance!—how brightly youthful the crisp hair under his light cap of helm,—how deftly curled the fringe of his horse's crest,—how vigorous in disciplined career of accustomed conquest, the two noble living creatures! This is Venetian fifteenth century work **of finest style.** Outside-of-house **work,** of course: **we** compare at present outside **work only,** panel with panel: but here are three hundred **years of** art progress written for you, **in** two pages,—from early thirteenth to late fifteenth century; and in this little bas-relief is all to be seen, that can be, of elementary principle, in the very crest and pride of Venetian sculpture,—of which **note** these following points.

First, the aspirations of the front of St. Mark's have been entirely achieved, and though the figure is still symbolical, it is now a symbol consisting in the most literal realization possible of natural facts. That is the way, if you **care to** see it, that **a** young knight rode, **in** 1480, or **thereabouts.** So, his foot was set in stirrup,—so his body borne,—so trim and true and orderly every thing in his harness and his life: and this rendered, observe, with the most consummate precision of artistic touch. Look at the strap of the stirrup,—at the little delicatest line of the spur,—can you think they are stone? don't they look like

leather and steel ? His flying mantle,—is it not silk more
than marble ? That is all in the beautiful doing of it:
precision first in exquisite sight of the thing itself, and
understanding **of the** qualities and signs, whether of silk
or steel ; and then, precision of touch, and cunning in use
of material, which it had taken three hundred years to
learn. Think what cunning there is in getting such edge
to the marble as will represent the spur line, or strap
leather, with such solid under-support that, **from** 1480 till
now, it stands rain and frost ! And for knowledge of
form,—look at the way the little princess's foot comes **out
under the drapery** as she shrinks back. Look at it first
from the left, to see how it is foreshortened, flat on the
rock ; then from the right, to see the curve of dress up
the limb :—think of the difference between this and the
feet of poor St. George Sartor of St. Mark's, pointed down
all their length. Finally, **see** how studious the whole
thing is of beauty **in every** part,—how it expects *you* also
to be studious. Trace the rich tresses of the princess's
hair, wrought where the figure melts into shadow ;—the
sharp edges of the **dragon's mail,** slipping over each other
as he wrings neck and coils tail ;—nay, what decorative
ordering and symmetry is even in the roughness of the
ground and rock ! And lastly, see how the whole piece
of work, to the simplest frame of it, must be by the sculptor's own hand : see how he breaks the line of his panel
moulding with the princess's hair, with St. George's helmet, with the rough ground itself at the base ;—the entire
tablet varied to its utmost edge, delighted in and ennobled
to its extreme limit of substance.

Here, then, as I said, is the top of Venetian sculpture-
art. Was there no going beyond this, think you ?

Assuredly, much beyond this the Venetian could have
gone, had he gone straight forward.   But at this point he
became perverse, and there is one sign of evil in this piece,
which you must carefully discern.

In the two earlier sculptures, of the sheep, and the
throned St. George, the artist never meant to say that
twelve sheep ever stood in two such rows, and were the
twelve apostles ; nor that St. George ever sat in that manner in a splendid chair.   But he entirely believed in the
facts of the lives of the apostles and saints, symbolized by
such figuring.

But the fifteenth century sculptor *does*, partly, mean
to assert that St. George did in that manner kill a dragon :
does not clearly know whether he did or not ; does not
care very much whether he did or not ;—thinks it will be
very nice if, at any rate, people believe that he did ;—but
is more bent, in the heart of him, on making a pretty bas-
relief than on any thing else.

Half way to infidelity, the fine gentleman is, with all
his dainty chiselling.   We will see, on those terms, what,
in another century, this fine chiselling comes to.

So now walk on, down the Merceria di San Salvador.
Presently, if it is morning, and the sky clear, you will see,
at the end of the narrow little street, the brick apse of St.
Saviour's, warm against the blue ; and, if you stand close
to the right, a solemn piece of old Venetian wall and window on the opposite side of the calle, which you might
pass under twenty times without seeing, if set on the
study of shops only.   Then you must turn to the right ;
perforce,—to the left again ; and now to the left, once
more ; and you are in the little piazza of St. Salvador,
with a building in front of you, now occupied as a fur-

niture store, which you will please look at with attention.

It reminds you of many things at home, I suppose?—
has a respectable, old-fashioned, city-of-London look about
it;—something of Greenwich Hospital, of Temple Bar, of
St. Paul's, of Charles the Second and the Constitution,
and the Lord Mayor and Mr. Bumble? Truly English, in
many respects, this solidly rich front of Ionic pillars, with
the four angels on the top, rapturously directing your attention, by the gracefullest gesticulation, to the higher
figure in the centre!

You have advanced another hundred and fifty years, and
are in mid seventeenth century. Here is the 'Progresso'
of Venice, exhibited to you, in consequence of her wealth,
and gay life, and advance in anatomical and other
sciences.

Of which, note first, the display of her knowledge of
angelic anatomy. Sabra, on the rock, just showed her
foot beneath her robe, and that only because she was
drawing back, frightened; but, here, every angel has his
petticoats cut up to his thighs; he is not sufficiently sacred
or sublime unless you see his legs so high.

Secondly, you see how expressive are their attitudes,—
"What a wonderful personage is this we have got in the
middle of us!"

That is Raphaelesque art of the finest. Raphael, by
this time, had taught the connoisseurs of Europe that
whenever you admire anybody, you open your mouth and
eyes wide; when you wish to show him to somebody else
you point at him vigorously with one arm, and wave the
somebody else on with the other; when you have nothing
to do of that sort, you stand on one leg and hold up the

other in a graceful line; these are the methods of true dramatic expression. Your drapery, meanwhile, is to be arranged in "sublime masses," and is not to be suggestive of any particular stuff!

If you study the drapery of these four angels thoroughly, you can scarcely fail of knowing, henceforward, what a bad drapery is, to the end of time. Here is drapery supremely, exquisitely bad; it is impossible, by any contrivance, to get it worse. Merely clumsy, ill-cut clothing, you may see any day; but there is skill enough in this to make it exemplarily execrable. That flabby flutter, wrinkled swelling, and puffed pomp of infinite disorder;—the only action of it, being blown up, and away; the only calm of it, collapse;—the resolution of every miserable fold not to fall, if it can help it, into any natural line,—the running of every lump of it into the next, as dough sticks to dough—remaining, not less, evermore incapable of any harmony or following of each other's lead or way;—and the total rejection of all notion of beauty or use in the stuff itself. It is stuff without thickness, without fineness, without warmth, without coolness, without lustre, without texture; not silk,—not linen,—not woollen;—something that wrings, and wrinkles, and gets between legs,—that is all. Worse drapery than this, you cannot see in mortal investiture.

Nor worse *want* of drapery, neither—for the legs are as ungraceful as the robes that discover them; and the breast of the central figure, whom all the angels admire, is packed under its corslet like a hamper of tomata apples.

To this type the Venetians have now brought their symbol of divine life in man. For this is also—St. Theodore! And the respectable building below, in the Bumble style, is the last effort of his school of Venetian gentlemen to house themselves respectably. With **Ionic** capitals, bare-legged angels, **and** the Dragon, now squareheaded and blunt-nosed, they **thus** contrive their last clubhouse, and prepare, for resuscitated Italy, **in** continued ' Progresso,' a stately furniture store. **Here you** may buy cruciform stools, indeed! and patent oilcloths, and other supports of your **Venetian** worshipful dignity, to heart's content. Here is your God's Gift to **the** nineteenth century. " **Deposito** mobili nazionali **ed esteri ; quadri ;** libri antichi e moderni, ed oggetti diversi."

Nevertheless, through all this decline in **power and** idea, there is yet, let us note finally, some wreck of Christian intention, some feeble coloring of Christian faith. A saint is still held to be an admirable person ; he is practically still the patron of your fashionable club-house, where you meet to offer him periodical prayer and alms. This architecture is, seriously, the best you can think of ; those angels **are** handsome, **according to** your notions of personality ; their attitudes really are such as you suppose to be **indicative of** celestial rapture,—their features, of celestial disposition.

We will see what change another fifty years will bring about in these faded feelings of Venetian soul.

The little calle on your right, as you front St. Theodore, will bring you straight to the quay below the Rialto, where your gondola shall be waiting, to take you as far as the bridge **over** the Cannareggio under the Palazzo Labia. Stay your gondola before passing under it, and look carefully at the sculptured ornaments of the arch, and then **at** the correspondent ones on the other side.

In these you see the last manner of sculpture, executed by Venetian artists, according to the mind of Venice, for her own pride and pleasure. Much she has done since, of art-work, to sell to strangers, executed as she thinks will please the *stranger* best. But of art produced for *her own* joy and in her own honor, this is a chosen example of the last !

Not representing saintly persons, you see ; nor angels in attitudes of admiration. Quite other personages than angelic, and with expressions of any thing rather than affection or respect for aught of good, in earth or heaven. Such were the last imaginations of her polluted heart, before death. She had it no more in her power to conceive any other. " Behold thy last gods,"—the Fates compel her thus to gaze and perish.

This last stage of her intellectual death precedes her political one by about a century ; during the last half of which, however, she did little more than lay foundations of walls which she could not complete. Virtually, we may close her national history with the seventeenth century ; we shall not ourselves follow it even so far.

I have shown you, to-day, pieces of her art-work by which you may easily remember its cardinal divisions.

You saw first the work of her Greek masters, under whom she learned both her faith and art.

Secondly, the beginning of her own childish efforts, in the St. George enthroned.

Thirdly, the culmination of her skill in the St. George combatant.

Fourthly, the languor of her faith and art power, under the advance of her luxury, in the hypocrisy of St. Theodore's Scuola, now a furniture warehouse.

Lastly, her dotage before shameful death.

In the next chapter, I will mark, by their natural limits, the epochs of her political history, which correspond to these conditions of her knowledge, hope, and imagination.

But as you return home, and again pass before the porches of St. Mark's, I may as well say at once what I can of these six bas-reliefs between them.

On the sides of the great central arch are St. George and St. Demetrius, so inscribed in Latin. Between the next lateral porches, the Virgin' and Archangel Gabriel, so inscribed,—the Archangel in Latin, the "Mother of God" in Greek.

And between these and the outer porches, uninscribed, two of the labors of Hercules. I am much doubtful concerning these, myself,—do not know their manner of sculpture, nor understand their meaning. They are fine work; the Venetian antiquaries say, very early (sixth century); types, it may be, of physical human power prevailing over wild nature; the war of the world before Christ.

Then the Madonna and Angel of Annunciation express the Advent.

Then the two Christian Warrior Saints express the heart of Venice in her armies.

There is no doubt, therefore, of the purposeful choosing and placing of these bas-reliefs. Where the outer ones were brought from, I know not; the four inner ones, I think, are all contemporary, and carved for their place by the Venetian scholars of the Greek schools, in late twelfth or early thirteenth century.

My special reason for assigning this origin to them is the manner of the foliage under the feet of the Gabriel, in which is the origin of **all** the early foliage in the Gothic of Venice. This bas-relief, however, appears **to** be by a better master than **the** others—perhaps later ; and is of extreme beauty.

Of **the ruder** St. George, and successive sculptures of Evangelists on the north side, I cannot yet speak with decision ; nor would you, until we have followed the story of Venice farther, probably **care to hear.**

CHAPTER V.

THE history of Venice, then, divides itself into four quite distinct periods.

I. The first, in which the fugitives from many cities on the mainland, gathered themselves into one nation, dependent for existence on its labor upon the sea; and which develops itself, by that labor, into a race distinct in temper from all the other families of Christendom. This process of growth and mental formation is necessarily a long one, the result being so great. It takes roughly, seven hundred years—from the fifth to the eleventh century, both inclusive. Accurately, from the Annunciation day, March 25th, 421, to the day of St. Nicholas, December 6th, 1100.

At the close of this epoch Venice had fully learned Christianity from the Greeks, chivalry from the Normans, and the laws of human life and toil from the ocean. Prudently and nobly proud, she stood, a helpful and wise princess, highest in counsel and mightiest in deed, among the knightly powers of the world.

II. The second period is that of her great deeds in war, and of the establishment of her reign in justice and truth (the best at least that she knew of either), over, nominally, the fourth part of the former Roman Empire. It includes the whole of the twelfth and thirteenth centuries, and is chiefly characterized by the religious passion of the Crusades. It lasts, in accurate terms, from December 6th, 1100, to February 28th, 1297; but as the event of that day was not confirmed till three years afterwards, we get the fortunately precise terminal date of 1301.

III. The third period is that of religious meditation, as distinct, though not withdrawn from, religious action. It is marked by the establishment of schools of kindly civil order, and by its endeavors to express, in word and picture, the thoughts which until then had wrought in silence. The entire body of her noble art-work belongs to this time. It includes the fourteenth and fifteenth centuries, and twenty years more : from 1301* to 1520.

IV. The fourth period is that of the luxurious use, and display, of the powers attained by the labor and meditation of former times, but now applied without either labor or meditation :—religion, art, and literature, having become things of custom and "costume." It spends, in eighty years, the fruits of the toil of a thousand, and terminates, strictly, with the death of Tintoret, in 1594 ; we will say 1600.

From that day the remainder of the record of Venice is only the diary of expiring delirium, and by those who love her, will be traced no farther. But while you are here within her walls I will endeavor to interpret clearly to you the legends on them, in which she has herself related the passions of her Four Ages.

And see how easily they are to be numbered and remembered. Twelve hundred years in all ; divided—if, broadly, we call the third period two centuries, and the

---

* Compare 'Stones of Venice' (old edit.), vol. ii., p. 291.

fourth, one,—in diminishing proportion, 7, 2, 2, 1 : it is like the spiral of a shell, reversed.

I have in this first sketch of them distinguished these four ages by the changes in the chief element of every nation's mind—its religion, with the consequent results upon its art.   But you see I have made no mention whatever of all that common historians think it their primal business to discourse of,—policy, government, commercial prosperity!   One of my dates however is determined by a crisis of internal policy ; and I will at least note, as the material instrumentation of the spiritual song, the metamorphoses of state-order which accompanied, in each transition, the new nativities of the state's heart.

I. During the first period, which completes the binding of many tribes into one, and the softening of savage faith into intelligent Christianity, we see the gradual establishment of a more and more distinctly virtuous monarchic authority ; continually disputed, and often abused, but purified by every reign into stricter duty, and obeyed by every generation with more sacred regard.   At the close of this epoch, the helpful presence of God, and the leading powers of the standard-bearer Saint, and sceptre-bearing King, are vitally believed ; reverently, and to the death, obeyed.   And, in the eleventh century, the Palace of the Duke and lawgiver of the people, and his Chapel, enshrining the body of St. Mark, stand, bright with marble and gold, side by side.

II. In the second period, that of active Christian warfare, there separates itself from the mass of the people, chiefly by pre-eminence in knightly achievement, and persistence in patriotic virtue,—but also, by the intellectual training received in the conduct of great foreign enterprise, and maintenance of legislation among strange people,—an order of aristocracy, raised both in wisdom and valor greatly above the average level of the multitude, and gradually joining to the traditions of Patrician Rome, the domestic refinements, and imaginative sanctities, of the northern and Frankish chivalry, whose chiefs were their battle comrades. At the close of the epoch, this more sternly educated class determines to assume authority in the government of the State, unswayed by the humor, and unhindered by the ignorance, of the lower classes of the people ; and the year which I have assigned for the accurate close of the second period is that of the great division between nobles and plebeians, called by the Venetians the "Closing of the Council,"—the restriction, that is to say, of the powers of the Senate to the lineal aristocracy.

III. The third period shows us the advance of this now separate body of Venetian gentlemen in such thought and passion as the privilege of their position admitted, or its temptations provoked. The gradually increasing knowledge of literature, culminating at last in the discovery of printing, and revival of classic formulæ of method, modified by reflection, or dimmed by disbelief, the frank Christian faith of earlier ages ; and social position independent of military prowess, developed at once the ingenuity, frivolity, and vanity of the scholar, with the avarice and cunning of the merchant.

Protected and encouraged by a senate thus composed, distinct companies of craftsmen, wholly of the people, gathered into vowed fraternities of social order ; and, retaining the illiterate sincerities of their religion, labored in unambitious peace, under the orders of the philosophic

aristocracy ;—built for them their great palaces, and overlaid their walls, within and without, with gold and purple
of Tyre, precious now in Venetian hands as the colors of
heaven more than of the sea.   By the hand of one of
them, the picture of Venice, with her nobles in her streets,
at the end of this epoch, is preserved to you as yet, and I
trust will be, by the kind fates, preserved datelessly.

IV. In the fourth period, the discovery of printing
having confused literature into vociferation, and the delicate skill of the craftsman having provoked splendor into
lasciviousness, the jubilant and coruscant passions of the
nobles, stately yet in the forms of religion, but scornful of
her discipline, exhausted, in their own false honor, at once
the treasures of Venice and her skill ; reduced at last her
people to misery, and her policy to shame, and smoothed
for themselves the downward way to the abdication of
their might for evermore.

Now these two histories of the religion and policy of
Venice are only intense abstracts of the same course of
thought and events in every nation of Europe.   Throughout the whole of Christendom, the two stories in like
manner proceed together.   The acceptance of Christianity
—the practice of it—the abandonment of it—and moral
ruin.   The development of kingly authority,—the obedience to it—the corruption of it—and social ruin.   But
there is no evidence that the first of these courses of
national fate is vitally connected with the second.   That
infidel kings may be just, and Christian ones corrupt, was
the first lesson Venice learned when she began to be a
scholar.

And observe there are three quite distinct conditions of
feeling and assumptions of theory in which we may ap-

proach this matter. The first, that of our numerous cockney friends,—that the dukes of Venice were mostly hyp-
ocrites, and if not, fools ; that their pious zeal was merely
such a cloak for their commercial appetite as modern church-
going is for modern swindling ; or else a pitiable halluci-
nation and puerility:—that really the attention of the
supreme cockney mind would be wasted on such bygone
absurdities, and that out of mere respect for the common
sense of monkey-born-and-bred humanity, the less we say
of them the better.

The second condition of feeling is, in its full confession,
a very rare one ;—that of true respect for the Christian
faith, and sympathy with the passions and imaginations it
excited, while yet in security of modern enlightenment,
the observer regards the faith itself only as an exquisite
dream of mortal childhood, and the acts of its votaries as
a beautifully deceived heroism of vain hope.

This theory of the splendid mendacity of Heaven, and
majestic somnambulism of man, I have only known to be
held in the sincere depth of its discomfort, by one of my
wisest and dearest friends, under the pressure of uncom-
prehended sorrow in his own personal experience. But
to some extent it confuses or undermines the thoughts of
nearly all men who have been interested in the material
investigations of recent physical science, while retaining
yet imagination and understanding enough to enter into
the heart of the religious and creative ages.

And it necessarily takes possession of the spirit of such
men chiefly at the times of personal sorrow, which teach
even to the wisest, the hollowness of their best trust, and
the vanity of their dearest visions ; and when the epitaph

of all human virtue, and sum of human peace, seem to be
written in the lowly argument,—

> " We are such stuff
> As dreams are made of ; and our little life
> Is rounded with a sleep."

The third, the only modest, and therefore the only rational, theory, is, that we are all and always, in these as
in former ages, deceived by our own guilty passions,
blinded by our own obstinate wills, and misled by the in-
solence and fantasy of our ungoverned thoughts ; but that
there is verily a Divinity in nature which has shaped the
rough hewn deeds of our weak human effort, and revealed
itself in rays of broken, but of eternal light, to the souls
which have desired to see the day of the Son of Man.

By the more than miraculous fatality which has been
hitherto permitted to rule the course of the kingdoms of this
world, the men who are capable of accepting such faith,
are rarely able to read the history of nations by its interpretation. They nearly all belong to some one of the
passionately egoistic sects of Christianity ; and are miserably perverted into the missionary service of their own
schism ; eager only, in the records of the past, to gather
evidence to the advantage of their native persuasion, and
to the disgrace of all opponent forms of similar heresy ;
or, that is to say, in every case, of nine-tenths of the religion of this world.

With no less thankfulness for the lesson, than shame
for what it showed, I have myself been forced to recognize the degree in which all my early work on Venetian
history was paralyzed by this petulance of sectarian ego-
tism ; and it is among the chief advantages I possess for

the task now undertaken in my closing years, that there
are few of the errors against which I have to warn my
readers, into which I have not myself at some time fallen.
Of which errors, the chief, and cause of all the rest, is the
leaning on our own understanding; the thought that we
can measure the hearts of our brethren, and judge of the
ways of God. Of the hearts of men, noble, yet " de-
ceitful above all things, who can know them ?"—that infinitely perverted scripture is yet infinitely true. And
for the ways of God ! Oh, my good and gentle reader,
how much otherwise would not you and I have made this
world ?

CHAPTER VI.

Not, therefore, to lean on our own sense, but in all the strength it has, to use it; not to be captives to our private thoughts, but to dwell in them, without wandering, until, out of the chambers of our own hearts we begin to conceive what labyrinth is in those of others,—thus we have to prepare ourselves, good reader, for the reading of any history.

If but we may at last succeed in reading a little of our own, and discerning what scene of the world's drama we are set to play in,—drama whose tenor, tragic or other, seemed of old to rest with so few actors; but now, with this pantomimic mob upon the stage, can you make out any of the story?—prove, even in your own heart, how much you believe that there is any Playwright behind the scenes?

Such a wild dream as it is!—nay, as it always has been, except in momentary fits of consciousness, and instants of startled spirit,—perceptive of heaven. For many centuries the Knights of Christendom wore their religion gay as their crest, familiar as their gauntlet, shook it high in the summer air, hurled it fiercely in other people's faces, grasped their spear the firmer for it, sat their horses the prouder; but it never entered into their minds for an instant to ask the meaning of it! 'Forgive us our sins:' by

all means—yes, and the next garrison that holds out a day
longer than is convenient to us, hang them every man to his
battlement. 'Give us this day our daily bread,'—'yes, and
our neighbor's also, if we have any luck. 'Our Lady and
the saints!' Is there any infidel dog that doubts of them?
—in God's name, boot and spur—and let us have the head
off him. It went on so, frankly and bravely, to the twelfth
century, at the earliest; when men begin to think in a
serious manner; more or less of gentle manners and domestic comfort being also then conceivable and attainable.
Rosamond is not any more asked to drink out of her
father's skull. Rooms begin to be matted and wainscoted;
shops to hold store of marvellous foreign wares; knights
and ladies learn to spell, and to read, with pleasure; music
is everywhere;—Death, also. Much to enjoy—much to
learn, and to endure—with Death always at the gates. "If
war fail thee in thine own country, get thee with haste
into another," says the faithful old French knight to the
boy-chevalier, in early fourteenth century days.

No country stays more than two centuries in this intermediate phase between Faith and Reason. In France
it lasted from about 1150 to 1350; in England, 1200 to
1400; in Venice, 1300 to 1500. The course of it is always in the gradual development of Christianity,—till
her yoke gets at once too aerial, and too straight, for the
mob, who break through it at last as if it were so much
gossamer; and at the same fatal time, wealth and luxury,
with the vanity of corrupt learning, foul the faith of the
upper classes, who now begin to wear their Christianity,
not tossed for a crest high over their armor, but stuck as
a plaster over their sores, inside of their clothes. Then
comes printing, and universal gabble of fools; gunpow-

der, and the end of all the noble methods of war; trade, and universal swindling; wealth, and universal gambling; idleness, and universal harlotry; and so at last—Modern Science and Political Economy; and the reign of St. Petroleum instead of St. Peter. Out of which God only knows what is to come next; but He *does* know, whatever the Jew swindlers and apothecaries' 'prentices think about it.

Meantime, with what remainder of belief in Christ may be left in us; and helping that remnant with all the power we have of imagining what Christianity was, to people who, without understanding its claims or its meaning, did not doubt for an instant its statements of fact, and used the whole of their childish imagination to realize the acts of their Saviour's life, and the presence of His angels, let us draw near to the first sandy thresholds .of the Venetian's home.

Before you read any of the so-called historical events of the first period, I want you to have some notion of their scene. Your will hear of Tribunes—Consuls—Doges; but what sort of tribes were they tribunes of? what sort of nation were they dukes of? You will hear of brave naval battle—victory over sons of Emperors: what manner of people were they, then, whose swords lighten thus brightly in the dawn of chivalry?

For the whole of her first seven-hundred years of work and war, Venice was in great part a wooden town; the houses of the noble mainland families being for long years chiefly at Heráclea, and on other islands; nor they magnificent, but farm-villas mostly, of which, and their farming, more presently. Far too much stress has been generally laid on the fishing and salt-works of early Venice, as if they were her only businesses; nevertheless at least you may be sure of this much, that for seven hundred years Venice had more likeness in her to old Yarmouth than to new Pall Mall; and that you might come to shrewder guess of what she and her people were like, by living for a year or two lovingly among the herring-catchers of Yarmouth Roads, or the boatmen of Deal or Boscastle, than by reading any lengths of eloquent history. But you are to know also, and remember always, that this amphibious city—this Phocæa, or sea-dog of towns—looking with soft human eyes at you from the sand, Proteus himself latent in the salt-smelling skin of her—had fields, and plots of garden here and there; and, far and near, sweet woods of Calypso, graceful with quivering sprays, for woof of nests—gaunt with forked limbs for ribs of ships; had good milk and butter from familiarly couchant cows; thickets wherein familiar birds could sing; and finally was observant of clouds and sky, as pleasant and useful phenomena. And she had at due distances among her simple dwellings, stately churches of marble.

These things you may know, if you will, from the following "quite ridiculous" tradition, which, ridiculous as it may be, I will beg you for once to read, since the Doge Andrea Dandolo wrote it for you, with the attention due to the address of a Venetian gentleman, and a King.*

"As head and bishop of the islands, the Bishop Mag-

---

* A more graceful form of this legend has been translated with feeling and care by the Countess Isobel Cholmley, in Bermani, from an MS. in her possession, copied, I believe, from one of the tenth century. But I take the form in which it was written by Andrea Dandolo, that the reader may have more direct associations with the beautiful image of the Doge on his tomb in the Baptistery.

nus of Altinum went from place to place to give them comfort, saying that they ought to thank God for having escaped from these barbarian cruelties. And there appeared to him St. Peter, ordering him that in the head of Venice, or truly of the city of Rivoalto, where he should find oxen and sheep feeding, he was to build a church under his (St. Peter's) name. And thus he did; building St. Peter's Church in the island of Olivolo, where at present is the seat and cathedral church of Venice.

" Afterwards appeared to him the angel Raphael, committing it to him, that at another place, where he should find a number of birds together, he should build him a church : and so he did, which is the church of the Angel Raphael in Dorsoduro.

" Afterwards appeared to him Messer Jesus Christ our Lord, and committed to him that in the midst of the city he should build a church, in the place, above which he should see a red cloud rest : and so he did; and it is San Salvador.

" Afterwards appeared to him the most holy Mary the Virgin, very beautiful ; and commanded him that where he should see a white cloud rest, he should build a church : which is the church of St. Mary the Beautiful.

" Yet still appeared to him St. John the Baptist, commanding that he should build two churches, one near the other—the one to be in his name, and the other in the name of his father. Which he did, and they are San Giovanni in Bragola, and San Zaccaria.

" Then appeared to him the apostles of Christ, wishing, they also, to have a church in this new city ; and they committed it to him that where he should see twelve cranes in a company, there he should build it. Lastly appeared to him the blessed Virgin Giustina, and ordered him that where he should find vines bearing fresh fruits there he should build her a church."

Now this legend is quite one of the most precious things in the story of Venice: preserved for us in this form at the end of the fourteenth century, by one of her most highly educated gentlemen, it shows the very heart of her religious and domestic power, and assures for us, with other evidence, these following facts.

First; that a certain measure of pastoral home-life was mingled with Venice's training of her sailors;—evidence whereof remains to this day, in the unfailing 'Campo' round every church; the church 'meadow'—not church-'yard.' It happened to me, once in my life, to go to church in a state of very great happiness and peace of mind; and this in a very small and secluded country church. And Fors would have it that I should get a seat in the chancel; and the day was sunny, and the little side chancel-door was open opposite into, what I hope was a field. I saw no graves in it; but in the sunshine, sheep feeding. And I never was at so divine a church service before, nor have been since. If you will read the opening of Wordsworth's 'White Doe of Rylstone,' and can enjoy it, you may learn from it what the look of an old Venetian church would be, with its surrounding field. St. Mark's Place was only the meadow of St. Theodore's church, in those days.

Next—you observe the care and watching of animals. That is still a love in the heart of Venice. One of the chief little worries to me in my work here, is that I walk faster than the pigeons are used to have people walk; and am continually like to tread on them; and see story in Fors, March of this year, of the gondolier and his dog. Nay, though, the other day, I was greatly tormented at the public gardens, in the early morning, when I had counted on a quiet walk, by a cluster of boys who were chasing the first twittering birds of the spring from bush to bush, and throwing sand at them, with wild shouts and whistles, they were not doing it, as I at first thought, in mere mischief, but with hope of getting a penny or two to gamble with, if they could clog the poor little creatures' wings enough to bring one down— "'Canta bene, signor, quell' uccellino." Such the nineteenth century's reward of Song. Meantime, among the silvery gleams of islet tower on the lagoon horizon, beyond Mazorbo—a white ray flashed from the place where St. Francis preached to the Birds.

Then thirdly—note that curious observance of the color of clouds. That is gone, indeed; and no Venetian, or Italian, or Frenchman, or Englishman, is likely to know or care, more, whether any God-given cloud is white or red; the primal effort of his entire human existence being now to vomit out the biggest black one he can pollute the heavens with. But, in their rough way, there was yet a perception in the old fishermen's eyes of the difference between white 'nebbia' on the morning sea, and red clouds in the evening twilight. And the Stella Maris comes in the sea Cloud;—Leucothea: but the Son of Man on the jasper throne.

Thus much of the aspect, and the thoughts of earliest Venice, we may gather from one tradition, carefully read. What historical evidence exists to confirm the gathering, you shall see in a little while; meantime—such being the

scene of the opening drama—we must next consider somewhat of the character of the actors. For though what
manner of houses they had, has been too little known,
what manner of men **they were, has** not at all been
known, or even the reverse of known,—belied.

CHAPTER VII.

DIVINE RIGHT.

ARE you impatient with me? and do you wish me, ceasing preamble, to begin—'In the year this, happened that,' and set you down a page of dates and Doges to be learned off by rote? You must be denied such delight a little while longer. If I begin dividing this first period, at present (and it has very distinctly articulated joints of its own), we should get confused between the subdivided and the great epochs. I must keep your thoughts to the Three Times, till we know them clearly; and in this chapter I am only going to tell you the story of a single Doge of the First Time, and gather what we can out of it.

Only, since we have been hitherto dwelling on the soft and religiously sentimental parts of early Venetian character, it is needful that I should ask you to notice one condition in their government of a quite contrary nature, which historians usually pass by as if it were of no consequence; namely, that during this first period, five Doges, after being deposed, had their eyes put out.

Pulled out, say some writers, and I think with evidence reaching down as far as the endurance on our English stage of the blinding of Gloster in King Lear.

But at all events the Dukes of Venice, whom her people thought to have failed in their duty, were in that manner incapacitated from reigning more.

An Eastern custom, as we know: grave in judgment;

in the perfectness of it, joined with infliction of grievous
Sight, before the infliction of grievous Blindness; that so
the last memory of this world's light might remain a
grief. "And they slew the sons of Zedekiah before his
eyes; and put out the eyes of Zedekiah."

Custom I know not how ancient. The sons of Eliab,
when Judah was young in her Exodus, like Venice,
appealed to it in their fury: "Is it a small thing that
thou hast brought us up out of a land that floweth with
milk and honey, except thou make thyself altogether a
Prince over us; wilt thou put out the eyes of these men?"

The more wild Western races of Christianity, early Irish
and the like,—Norman even, in the pirate times,—inflict
the penalty with reckless scorn; * but Venice deliberately,
as was her constant way; such her practical law against
leaders whom she had found spiritually blind: "These, at
least, shall guide no more."

Very savage! monstrous! if you will; whether it be
not a worse savageness deliberately to follow leaders *without* sight, may be debatable.

The Doge whose history I am going to tell you was the
last of deposed Kings in the first epoch. Not blinded,

---

* Or sometimes pitifully: "Olaf was by no means an unmerciful
man,—much the reverse where he saw good cause. There was a
wicked old King Rærik, for example, one of those five kinglets whom,
with their bits of armaments, Olaf, by stratagem, had surrounded one
night, and at once bagged and subjected when morning rose, all of
them consenting;—all of them except this Rærik, whom Olaf, as the
readiest sure course, took home with him; blinded, and kept in his
own house, finding there was no alternative but that or death to the
obstinate old dog, who was a kind of distant cousin withal, and could
not conscientiously be killed "—(Carlyle,—' Early Kings of Norway,'
p. 121)—conscience, and kin-ship, or " kindliness," declining somewhat in the Norman heart afterwards.

he, as far as I read: but permitted, I trust peaceably, to
become a monk; Venice owing to him much that has been
the delight of her own and other people's eyes, ever since.
Respecting the occasion of his dethronement, a story
remains, however, very notably in connection with this
manner of punishment.

Venice, throughout this first period in close alliance
with the Greeks, sent her Doge, in the year 1082, with a
"valid fleet, terrible in its most ordered disposition," to
defend the Emperor Alexis against the Normans, led by
the greatest of all Western captains, Guiscard.

The Doge defeated him in naval battle once; and, on
the third day after, once again, and so conclusively, that,
thinking the debate ended, he sent his lightest ships
home, and anchored on the Albanian coast with the rest,
as having done his work.

But Guiscard, otherwise minded on that matter, with
the remains of his fleet,—and his Norman temper at
hottest,—attacked him for the third time. The Greek
allied ships fled. The Venetian ones, partly disabled, had
no advantage in their seamanship: * question only remained, after the battle, how the Venetians should bear
themselves as prisoners. Guiscard put out the eyes of
some; then, with such penalty impending over the rest,
demanded that they should make peace with the Normans, and fight for the Greek Emperor no more.

But the Venetians answered, "Know thou, Duke
Robert, that although also *we should see our wives and
children slain*, we will not deny our covenants with the

---

* Their crews had eaten all their **stores**, and their ships **were flying**
ight, and would not steer **well**.

Autocrat Alexis; neither will we cease to help him, and to fight for him with our whole hearts."

The Norman chief sent them home unransomed.

There is a highwater mark for you of the waves of Venetian and Western chivalry in the eleventh century. A very notable scene; the northern leader, without rival the greatest soldier of the sea whom our rocks and ice-bergs bred: of the Venetian one, and his people, we will now try to learn the character more perfectly,—for all this took place towards the close of the Doge Selvo's life. You shall next hear what I can glean of the former course of it.

In the year 1053, the Abbey of St. Nicholas, the protector of mariners, had been built at the entrance of the port of Venice (where, north of the bathing establishment, you now see the little church of St. Nicholas of the Lido); the Doge Domenico Contarini, the Patriarch of Grado, and the Bishop of Venice, chiefly finding the funds for such edifice.

When the Doge Contarini died, the entire multitude of the people of Venice came in armed boats to the Lido, and the Bishop of Venice, and the monks of the new abbey of St. Nicholas, joined with them in prayer,—the monks in their church and the people on the shore and in their boats,—that God would avert all dangers from their country, and grant to them such a king as should be worthy to reign over it. And as they prayed, with one accord, suddenly there rose up among the multitude the cry, "Domenico Selvo, we will, and we approve," whom a crowd of the nobles brought instantly forward thereupon, and raised him on their own shoulders and carried him to his boat; into which when he had entered, he put off his shoes from his feet, that he might in all humility

approach the church of St. Mark. And while the boats
began to row from the island towards Venice, the monk
who saw this, and tells us of it, himself began to sing the
Te Deum. All around, the voices of the people took up
the hymn, following it with the Kyrie Eleison, with such
litany keeping time to their oars in the bright noonday,
and rejoicing on their native sea ; all the towers of the
city answering with triumph peals as they drew nearer.
They brought their Doge to the Field of St. Mark, and
carried him again on their shoulders to the porch of the
church ; there, entering barefoot, with songs of praise to
God round him—"such that it seemed as if the vaults
must fall,"—he prostrated himself on the earth, and gave
thanks to God and St. Mark, and uttered such vow as was
in his heart to offer before them. Rising, he received at
the altar the Venetian sceptre, and thence entering the
Ducal Palace, received there the oath of fealty from the
people.*

* This account of the election of the Doge Selvo is given by Sansovino (' Venetia descritta,' Lib. xi. 40 ; Venice, 1663, p. 477),—saying at
the close of it simply, " Thus writes Domenico Rino, who was his chap-
lain, and who was present at what I have related." Sansovino seems
therefore to have seen Rino's manuscript : but Romanin, without
referring to Sansovino, gives the relatión as if he had seen the MS.
himself, but misprints the chronicler's name as Domenico *T*ino, causing
no little trouble to my kind friend Mr. Lorenzi and me, in hunting at
St. Mark's and the Correr Museum for the unheard-of chronicle, till
Mr. Lorenzi traced the passage. And since Sansovino's time nothing
has been seen or further said of the Rino Chronicle.—See Foscarini,
"della letteratura Veneziana," Lib. ii.

Romanin has also amplified and inferred somewhat beyond Sansovino's words. The dilapidation of the palace furniture, especially, is
not attributed by Sansovino to festive pillage, but to neglect after Contarini's death. Unquestionably, however, the custom alluded to in the
text existed from very early times

Benighted wretches, all of them, you think, prince
and people alike, don't you? They were pleasanter
creatures to see, at any rate, than any you will see in St.
Mark's field nowadays. If the pretty ladies, indeed,
would walk in the porch like the Doge, barefoot, instead
of in boots cloven in two like the devil's hoofs, something
might be said for them; but though they will recklessly
drag their dresses through it, I suppose they would
scarcely care to walk, like Greek maids, in that mixed
mess of dust and spittle with which modern progressive
Venice anoints her marble pavement. Pleasanter to look
at, I can assure you, this multitude delighting in their
God and their Duke, than these, who have no Paradise to
trust to with better gifts for them than a gazette, cigar,
and pack of cards; and no better governor than their own
wills. You will see no especially happy or wise faces
produced in St. Mark's Place under these conditions.

Nevertheless, the next means that the Doge Selvo took
for the pleasure of his people on his coronation day sa-
voured somewhat of modern republican principles. He
gave them "the pillage of his palace"—no less! Whatever they could lay their hands on, these faithful ones,
they might carry away with them, with the Doge's blessing. At evening he laid down the uneasy crowned head
of him to rest in mere dismantled walls; hands dexterous
in the practices of profitable warfare having bestirred
themselves all the day. Next morning the first Ducal
public orders were necessarily to the upholsterers and
furnishers for readornment of the palace-rooms. Not by
any special grace this, or benevolent novelty of idea in
the good Doge, but a received custom, hitherto; sacred
enough, if one understands it,—a kind of mythical putting

off all the burdens of one's former wealth, and entering barefoot, bare-body, bare-soul, into this one duty of Guide and Lord, lightened thus of all regard for his own affairs or properties. "Take all I have, from henceforth; the corporal vestments of me, and all that is in their pockets, I give you to-day; the stripped life of **me** is yours forever." Such, virtually, the King's vow.

Frankest largesse thus cast to his electors (modern bribery is quite as costly and not half so merry), the Doge set himself **to refit, not his own** palace merely, but much **more,** God's house: **for this** prince is one who has at once **David's piety,** and soldiership, and Solomon's love of fine **things; a** perfect man, as I read him, capable at once and gentle, religious and joyful, in the extreme: as a warrior the match of Robert Guiscard, who, you will find, was the soldier *par excellence* of the middle ages, but not his match in the wild-cat cunning—both of them alike in knightly honor, word being given. **As a** soldier, I say, the match of Guiscard, but not holding war for the pastime of life, still less for the duty of Venice or **her** king. Peaceful affairs, the justice and the **joy of** human deeds —in these he sought his power, by principle and passion equally; **religious,** as we have seen; royal, as we shall presently see; commercial, as we shall finally see; a perfect man, recognized as such with concurrent applause of people and submission of noble: "Domenico Selvo, we will, and we approve."

No flaw in him, then? Nay; "how bad the best of us!" say *Punch,** and the modern evangelical. Flaw he had,

---

* Epitaph on the Bishop of Winchester (Wilberforce); see Fors XLII., p. 125.

such as wisest men are not unliable to, with the strongest
—Solomon, Samson, Hercules, Merlin the Magician.

Liking pretty things, how could he help liking pretty
ladies? He married a Greek maid, who came with new
and strange light on Venetian eyes, and left wild fame of
herself: how, every morning, she sent her handmaidens to
gather the dew for her to wash with, waters of earth being
not pure enough. So, through lapse of fifteen hundred
years, descended into her Greek heart that worship in the
Temple of the Dew.

Of this queen's extreme luxury, and the miraculousness
of it in the eyes of simple Venice, many traditions are
current among later historians; which, nevertheless, I
find resolve themselves, on closer inquiry, into an appalled
record of the fact that she would actually not eat her meat
with her fingers, but applied it to her mouth with " certain
two-pronged instruments "* (of gold, indeed, but the
luxurious sin, in Venetian eyes, was evidently not in the
metal, but the fork); and that she indulged herself greatly
in the use of perfumes : especially about her bed, for
which whether to praise her, as one would an English
housewife for sheets laid up in lavender, or to cry haro
upon her, as the "stranger who flattereth," † I know
not, until I know better the reason of the creation of per-
fume itself, and of its use in Eastern religion and delight
—"All thy garments smell of myrrh, aloes, and cassia, out
of the ivory palaces whereby thou hast made me glad "—
fading and corrupting at last into the incense of the mass,
and the *extrait de Mille-fleurs* of Bond Street. What I do

* Cibos digitis non tangebat, sed quibusdam fuscinulis aureis et
bidentibus suo ori applicabat." (Petrus Damianus, quoted by Dandolo.)
† Proverbs vii., 5 and 17.

know is, that there was no more sacred sight to me, in ancient Florence, than the Spezieria of the Monks of Santa Maria Novella, with its precious vials of sweet odors, each illuminated with the little picture of the flower from which it had truly been distilled—and yet, that, in its loaded air one remembered that the flowers had grown in the fields of the Decameron.

But this also I know, and more surely, that the beautiful work done in St. Mark's during the Greek girl's reign in Venice first interpreted to her people's hearts, and made legible to their eyes, the law of Christianity in its eternal harmony with the laws of the Jew and of the Greek: and gave them the glories of Venetian art in true inheritance from the angels of that Athenian Rock, above which Ion spread his starry tapestry,* and under whose shadow his mother had gathered the crocus in the dew.

----

* I have myself learned more of the real meaning of Greek myths from Euripides than from any other Greek writer, except Pindar. But I do not at present know of any English rhythm interpreting him rightly—these poor sapless measures must serve my turn—(Wodhull's: 1778.)

" The sacred tapestry
Then taking from the treasures of the God,
He cover'd o'er the whole, a wondrous sight
To all beholders : first he o'er the roof
Threw robes, which Hercules, the son of Jove,
To Phœbus at his temple brought, the spoils
Of vanquished Amazons ;
On which these pictures by the loom were wrought ;
Heaven in its vast circumference all the stars
Assembling ; there his courses too the Sun
Impetuous drove, till ceas'd his waning flame,
And with him drew in his resplendent train,

Vesper's clear light ; then clad in sable garb
Night hasten'd ; hastening stars accompanied
Their Goddess ; through mid-air the Pleiades,
And with his falchion arm'd, Orion mov'd.
But the sides he covered
With yet more tapestry, the Barbaric fleet
To that of Greece opposed, was there display'd ;
Follow'd **a monstrous brood**, half horse, half man,
The Thracian monarch's furious steeds subdu'd,
And lion of Nemæa."

.   .   .   .

"   .   .   . Underneath those craggy rocks,
North of Minerva's citadel (the kings
Of Athens call them Macra),   .   .   .
Thou cam'st, resplendent with thy golden hair,
As I the crocus gathered, in my robe
Each vivid flower assembling, to compose
Garlands of fragrance."

The composition of fragrant garlands out of crocuses being however
Mr. Michael **Wodhull**'s improvement on Euripides. **Creusa**'s words are
literally, " Thou camest, thy hair flashing with gold, **as** I let fall the
crocus petals, gleaming gold back again, into my robe at my bosom."
Into the folds of it, across her breast ; as an English girl would have
let them fall into her lap.

CHAPTER VIII.

1. As I re-read the description I gave, thirty years since, of St. Mark's Church ;—much more as I remember, forty years since, and before, the first happy hour spent in trying to paint a piece of it, with my six-o'clock breakfast on the little café table beside me on the pavement in the morning shadow, I am struck, almost into silence, by wonder at my own pert little Protestant mind, which never thought for a moment of asking what the Church had been built for !

Tacitly and complacently assuming that I had had the entire truth of God preached to me in Beresford Chapel in the Walworth Road,—recognizing no possible Christian use or propriety in any other sort of chapel elsewhere ; and perceiving, in this bright phenomenon before me, nothing of more noble function than might be in some new and radiant sea-shell, thrown up for me on the sand ;—nay, never once so much as thinking, of the fair shell itself, "Who built its domed whorls, then ?" or "What manner of creature lives in the inside ?" Much less ever asking, "Who is lying dead therein ?"

2. A marvellous thing—the Protestant mind ! Don't think I speak as a Roman Catholic, good reader : I am a mere wandering Arab, if that will less alarm you, seeking but my cup of cold water in the desert ; and I speak only

as an Arab, or an Indian,—with faint hope of ever seeing
the ghost of Laughing Water. A marvellous thing, nevertheless, I repeat,—this Protestant mind! Down in
Brixton churchyard, all the fine people lie inside railings,
and their relations expect the passers-by to acknowledge
reverently who's *there:*—nay, only last year, in my own
Cathedral churchyard of Oxford, I saw the new grave of
a young girl fenced about duly with carved stone, and
overlaid with flowers; and thought no shame to kneel for
a minute or two at the foot of it,—though there were several good Protestant persons standing by.

But the old leaven is yet so strong in me that I am very
shy of being caught by any of my country people kneeling near St. Mark's grave.

"Because—you know—it's all nonsense: it isn't St.
Mark's—and never was,"—say my intellectual English
knot of shocked friends.

I suppose one must allow much to modern English zeal
for genuineness in all commercial articles. Be it so.
Whether God ever gave the Venetians what they thought
He had given, does not matter to us; He gave them at
least joy and peace in their imagined treasure, more than
we have in our real ones.

And he gave them the good heart to build this chapel
over the cherished grave, and to write on the walls of it,
St. Mark's gospel, for all eyes,—and, so far as their power
went, for all time.

3. But it was long before I learned to read that; and
even when, with Lord Lindsay's first help, I had begun
spelling it out,—the old Protestant palsy still froze my
heart, though my eyes were unsealed; and the preface to
the Stones of Venice was spoiled, in the very centre of its

otherwise good work by that blunder, which I've left standing in all its shame, and with its hat off—like **Dr.** Johnson repentant in Lichfield Market,—only putting the **note** to it " Fool that **I** was ! " (page **11**).* I fancied actually that the main function of **St.** Mark's was no more than of our St. George's at Windsor, **to be** the private chapel of the king and his knights ;—a blessed function that also, but how much lower than the other ?

4. " Chiesa Ducale." It never **entered my heart** once to think that there **was** a greater Duke than her Doge, for **Venice ;** and that she built, for her two Dukes, each their palace, side by side. The palace of the living, and of the,—Dead,—was he then—the other Duke ?

" Viva san Marco."

You wretched little cast-iron gaspipe of a cockney that you are, who insist that your soul's your own, (see " Punch " for 15th March, 1879, on the duties of Lent,) as if anybody else would ever care to have it ! is there yet **life** enough in the molecules, and plasm, and general mess of the making of you, to feel for an instant what that cry once meant, upon the lips of men ?

Viva, Italia ! you may still hear that cry sometimes, though she lies **dead** enough. Viva, Vittor—Pisani !— perhaps also that cry, yet again.

But the answer,—" Not Pisani, but St. Mark," when will you hear *that* again, nowadays ? Yet when those

---

* Scott himself (God knows I say it sorrowfully, and not to excuse my own error, but to prevent *his* from doing more mischief,) has made just the same mistake, but more grossly and fatally, in the character given to the Venetian Procurator in the " Talisman." His error is more shameful, because he has confused the institutions of Venice in the fifteenth century with those of the twelfth.

bronze horses were won by the Bosphorus, it was St.
Mark's standard, not Henry Dandolo's, that was first
planted on the tower of Byzantium,—and men believed—
by his own hand.   While yet his body lay here at rest : and
this, its requiem on the golden scroll, was then already
written over it—in Hebrew, and Greek, and Latin.

In Hebrew, by the words of the prophets of Israel.

In Greek, by every effort of the building labourer's
hand, and vision to his eyes.

In Latin, with the rhythmic verse which Virgil had
taught,—calm as the flowing of Mincio.

But if you will read it, you must understand now, once
for all, the method of utterance in Greek art,—here, and
in Greece, and in Ionia, and the isles, from its first days
to this very hour.

5. I gave you the bas-relief of the twelve sheep and little caprioling lamb for a general type of all Byzantine art,
to fix in your mind at once, respecting it, that its intense
first character is symbolism.   The thing represented means
more than itself,—is a sign, or letter, more than an image.

And this **is true**, not of Byzantine art only, but of all
Greek art, pur **sang**.   **Let** us leave, to-day, the narrow
and degrading word " Byzantine."   There is but one
Greek school, from Homer's day down to the Doge
Selvo's; and these St. Mark's mosaics are as truly wrought
in the **power of** Daedalus, with the Greek constructive
instinct, **and** in the **power of** Athena, with the Greek religious soul, as ever chest of Cypselus or shaft of Erech-
theum.   And therefore, whatever is represented here, be
it flower or rock, animal or man, means more than it is in
itself.   Not sheep, these twelve innocent woolly things,—
but the twelve voices of the gospel of heaven ;—not palm-

trees, these shafts of shooting stem and beaded fruit,—
but the living grace of God in the heart, springing up in
joy at Christ's coming ;—not a king, merely, this crowned
creature in his sworded state,—but the justice of God in
His eternal Law ;—not a queen, nor a maid only, this
Madonna in her purple shade,—but the love of God
poured forth, in the wonderfulness that passes the love of
woman. *She* may forget—yet will I not forget thee.

6. And in this function of his art, remember, it does
not matter to **the Greek** **how** far his image be *perfect* **or**
not. That it should be *understood* is enough,—if it can
be beautiful also, well ; but its function is not beauty, but
instruction. You cannot have purer examples of Greek
art than the drawings on any good vase of the Maratho-
nian time. Black figures on a red ground,—a few white
scratches through them, marking the joints of their
armour or the folds of their robes,—white circles for
eyes,—pointed pyramids for beards,—you don't suppose
that in these the Greek workman thought he had given
the likeness of gods ? Yet here, to his imagination, were
Athena, Poseidon, and Herakles,—and all the powers that
guarded his land, and cleansed his soul, and led him in
the way everlasting.

7. And the wider your knowledge extends over the distant days and homes of sacred art, the more constantly
and clearly you will trace the rise of its symbolic function,
from the rudest fringe of racing deer, or couchant leo-
pards, scratched on some ill-kneaded piece of clay, when
men had yet scarcely left their own cave-couchant life,—
up to the throne of Cimabue's Madonna. All forms, and
ornaments, and images, have a moral meaning as a nat-
ural one. Yet out of all, a restricted number, chosen for

an alphabet, are recognized always as given letters, of
which the familiar scripture is adopted by generation
after generation.

8. You had best begin reading the scripture of St.
Mark's on the low cupolas of the baptistery,—entering, as
I asked you many a day since, to enter, under the tomb
of the Doge Andrea Dandolo.

You see, the little chamber consists essentially of two
parts, each with its low cupola : one containing the Font,
the other the Altar.

The one is significant of Baptism with water unto re-
pentance.

The other of Resurrection to newness of life.

Burial, in baptism with water, of the lusts of the flesh.
Resurrection, in baptism by the spirit—here, and now, to
the beginning of life eternal.

Both the cupolas have Christ for their central figure :
surrounded, in that over the font, by the Apostles baptizing with water ; in that over the altar, surrounded by the
Powers of Heaven, baptizing with the Holy Ghost and
with fire.   Each of the Apostles, over the font, is seen
baptizing in the country to which he is sent.

Their legends, written above them, begin over the door of
entrance into the church, with St. John the Evangelist,
and end with St. Mark—the order of all being as follows :—

St. John the Evangelist baptizes in Ephesus.
St. James _____ Judæa.
St. Philip _____ Phrygia.
St. Matthew _____ Ethiopia.
St. Simon _____ Egypt.
St. Thomas _____ India.

St. Andrew_____ Achaia.
St. Peter _____ Rome.
St. Bartholomew (legend indecipherable).
St. Thaddeus _____ Mesopotamia.
St. Matthias _____ Palestine.
St. Mark _____ Alexandria.

Over the door is Herod's feast. Herodias' daughter dances with St. John Baptist's head in the charger, on her head,—simply the translation of any Greek maid on a Greek vase, bearing a pitcher of water on her head.

I am not sure, but I believe the picture is meant to represent the two separate times of Herod's dealing with St. John ; and that the figure at the end of the table is in the former time, St. John saying to him, " It is not lawful for thee to have her."

9. Pass on now into the farther chapel under the darker dome.

Darker, and very dark ;—to my old eyes, scarcely decipherable ;—to yours, if young and bright, it should be beautiful, for it is indeed the origin of all those golden-domed backgrounds of Bellini, and Cima, and Carpaccio; itself a Greek vase, but with new Gods. That ten-winged cherub in the recess of it, behind the altar, has written on the circle on its breast, " Fulness of Wisdom." It is the type

SCIENTIE + PLENITUDO

4*

of the Breath of the Spirit. But it was once a Greek Harpy, and its wasted limbs remain, scarcely yet clothed with flesh from the claws of birds that they were.

At the sides of it are the two powers of the Seraphim and Thrones: the Seraphim with sword; the Thrones (TRONIS), with *Fleur-de-lys* sceptre,—lovely.

Opposite, on the arch by which you entered are The Virtues, (VIRTUTES).

A dead body lies under a rock, out of which spring two torrents—one of water, one of fire. The Angel of the Virtues calls on the dead to rise.

Then the circle is thus completed:

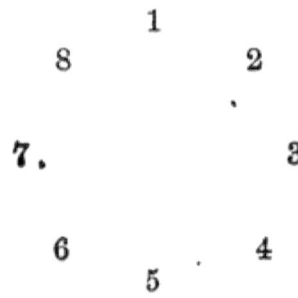

1, being the Wisdom angel; 8, the Seraphim; 2, the Thrones; and 5, the Virtues. 3. Dominations. 4. Angels. 6, Potentates. 7. Princes: the last with helm and sword.

Above, Christ Himself ascends, borne in a whirlwind of angels; and, as the vaults of Bellini and Carpaccio are only the amplification of the Harpy-Vault, so the Paradise of Tintoret is only the final fulfilment of the thought in this narrow cupola.

10. At your left hand, as you look towards the altar, is the most beautiful symbolic design of the Baptist's death that I know in Italy. Herodias is enthroned, not merely

as queen at Herod's table, but high and alone, the type of the Power of evil in pride of womanhood, through the past and future world, until Time shall be no longer.

On her right hand is St. John's execution; on her left, the Christian disciples, marked by their black crosses, bear his body to the tomb.

It is a four-square canopy, round arched; of the exact type of that in the museum at Perugia, given to the ninth century; but that over Herodias is round-trefoiled, and there is no question but that these mosaics are not earlier than the thirteenth century.

And yet they are still absolutely Greek in all modes of thought, and forms of tradition. The Fountains of fire and water are merely forms of the Chimera and the Peirene; and the maid dancing, though a princess of the thirteenth century in sleeves of ermine, is yet the phantom of some sweet water-carrier from an Arcadian spring.

11. These mosaics are the only ones in the interior of the church which belong to the time (1204) when its façade was completed by the placing of the Greek horses over its central arch, and illumined by the lovely series of mosaics still represented in Gentile Bellini's pictures, of which only one now remains. That *one*, left nearly intact —as Fate has willed—represents the church itself so completed; and the bearing of the body of St. Mark into its gates, with all the great kings and queens who have visited his shrine, standing to look on; not conceived, mind you, as present at any actual time, but as always looking on in their hearts.

12. I say it is left *nearly* intact. The three figures on the extreme right are restorations; and if the reader will

carefully study the difference between these and the rest; and note how all the faults of the old work are caricatured, and every one of its beauties lost—so that the faces which in the older figures are grave or sweet, are in these three new ones as of staring dolls,—he will know, once for all, what kind of thanks he owes to the tribe of Restorers— here and elsewhere.

Please note, farther, that at this time the church had round arches in the second story, (of which the shells exist yet,) but no pinnacles or marble fringes. All that terminal filigree is of a far later age. I take the façade as you see it stood—just after 1204—thus perfected. And I will tell you, so far as I know, the meaning of it, and of what it led to, piece by piece.

13. I begin with the horses,—those I saw in my dream in 1871,—"putting on their harness." See "Ariadne Florentina," p. 203.

These are the sign to Europe of the destruction of the Greek Empire by the Latin. They are chariot horses— the horses of the Greek quadriga,—and they were the trophies of Henry Dandolo. That is all you need know of them just now;—more, I hope, hereafter; but you must learn the meaning of a Greek quadriga first. They stand on the great outer archivolt of the façade: its ornaments, to the front, are of leafage closing out of spirals into balls interposed between the figures of eight Prophets (or Patriarchs?)—Christ in their midst on the keystone. No one would believe at first it was thirteenth-century work, so delicate and rich as it looks; nor is there anything else like it that I know, in Europe, of the date:—but pure thirteenth-century work it is, of rarest chiselling. I have cast two of its balls with their surrounding leafage, for St.

George's Museum; the most instructive pieces of sculpture of all I can ever show there.

14. Nor can you at all know how good it is, unless you **will** learn to draw: but some things concerning it may be seen, by attentive eyes, which are worth the dwelling upon.

You see, in the first place, that the outer foliage is all of one kind—pure Greek Acanthus,—not in the least transforming itself into ivy, or kale, **or rose**: trusting wholly for its **beauty to the** varied play **of its own** narrow and pointed lobes.

Narrow and pointed—but not jagged; for the jagged form **of** Acanthus, look at the two Jean d'Acre columns, **and return** to this—you will then feel why **I** call it *pure;* it is as nearly as possible the acanthus of early Corinth, only more flexible, and with more incipient blending of the character of the vine which **is used for** the central bosses. You see that **each leaf of** these last touches with its point a stellar knot of inwoven braid ; (compare the ornament round the low archivolt **of the porch** on your right below), **the** outer acanthus folding all in spiral whorls.

15. Now all thirteenth-century ornament of every nation runs much into spirals, and Irish and Scandinavian earlier decoration into little else. But these spirals are different from theirs. The Northern spiral is always elastic—like **that** of a watch-spring. The Greek spiral, drifted like that **of a** whirlpool, or whirlwind. It is always an eddy or vortex—not a living rod, like the point of a young fern.

At least, not living **its own** life—but under another life. It is under the power of the Queen of the Air; the power

also that is over the Sea, and over the human mind. The
first leaves I ever **drew** from St. Mark's were those drifted
under the breathing of it;* these on its uppermost cornice, far lovelier, are the final perfection of the Ionic
spiral, and of the thought in the temple of the Winds.

But perfected under a new influence. I said there was
nothing like them (that I knew) in European architecture.
But there is, in Eastern. They are only the amplification
of the cornice over the arches of the Holy Sepulchre at
Jerusalem.

16. I have been speaking hitherto of the front of the
arch only. Underneath it, the sculpture is equally rich,
and much more animated. **It** represents,—What think
you, or what would you have, good reader, if you were
yourself designing the central archivolt of your native
city, to companion, and even partly to sustain, the stones
on which those eight Patriarchs were carved—and
Christ?

The great men of your city, I suppose,—or the good
women of it? or the squires round about it? with the
Master of the hounds in the middle? or the Mayor and
Corporation? Well. That last guess comes near the
Venetian mind, only it is not my Lord Mayor, in his robes
of state, nor the Corporation at their city feast; but. the
mere Craftsmen of Venice—the Trades, that is to say, de-
pending on handicraft, beginning with the shipwrights,
and going on to the givers of wine and bread—ending
with the carpenter, the smith, and the fisherman.

Beginning, I say, if read from left to right, (north to
south,) **with the** shipwrights; **but** under them is a sitting

* See the large plate of two capitals in early folio illustrations.

figure, though sitting, yet supported by crutches. I cannot read this symbol : one may fancy many meanings in it,—but I do not trust fancy in such matters. Unless I know what a symbol means, I do not tell you my own thoughts of it.

17. If, however, we read from right to left, Orientalwise, the order would be more intelligible. It is then thus :

1. Fishing.
2. Forging.
3. Sawing.   Rough carpentry ?
4. Cleaving wood with axe.   Wheelwright ?
5. Cask and tub making.
6. Barber-surgery.
7. Weaving.
  Keystone—Christ *the Lamb ;* i.e., in humiliation.
8. Masonry.
9. Pottery.
10. The Butcher.
11. The Baker.
12. **The Vintner.**
13. The Shipwright.   **And**
14. The rest of old age ?

18. But it is not here the place to describe these carvings to you,—there are none others like them in Venice except the bases of the piazzetta shafts ; and there is little work like them elsewhere, pure realistic sculpture of the twelfth and thirteenth centuries : I may have much to say of them in their day—not now.

Under these labourers you may read, in large letters, a piece of history from the Vienna Morning Post—or whatever the paper was—of the year 1815, with which we are not concerned, **nor** need anybody else be so, to the end of time.

Not with that; nor with the mosaic of the vault beneath —flaunting glare of **Venetian art in its ruin.** No vestige of old work remains till we come to those steps of stone **ascending** on each side over the inner archivolt; a strange method of **enclosing its curve ;** but done **with special purpose.** If you look in the Bellini **picture, you** will see that **these steps** formed the **rocky** midst of a mountain **which** rose over them for the ground, in the old mosaic; the Mount of the Beatitudes. And on the vault above, stood **Christ blessing for** ever—not as standing on the Mount, **but supported above it by Angels.**

19. And on the archivolt itself were carved the Virtues —with, it is said, the Beatitudes; but I am not sure **yet** of anything **in this** archivolt, except that it is entirely splendid twelfth-century **sculpture.** I had the separate figures cast for **my** English museum, and put off the ex-**amination of them when I** was overworked. The Forti-**tude, Justice,** Faith, and Temperance are clear enough on **the right—and** the keystone figure is Constancy, **but I am sure of nothing** else **yet :** the less that interpretation partly depended on the scrolls, of which the letters were gilded, not carved :—the figures also gilded, in Bellini's time.

Then the innermost archivolt of all is of mere twelfth-century grotesque, unworthy of its place. But there were **so** many entrances to the atrium that the builders did not care to trust special teaching to any one, even the central, **except as a part of the façade. The** atrium, or outer cloister itself, **was the** real porch of the temple. And *that* they covered with as close scripture as they could

—the whole Creation and Book of Genesis pictured on it.

20. These are the mosaics usually attributed to the Doge Selvo: I cannot myself date any mosaics securely with precision, never having studied the technical structure of them; and these also are different from the others of St. Mark's in being more Norman than Byzantine in manner; and in an ugly admittance and treatment of nude form, which I find only elsewhere in manuscripts of the tenth and eleventh centuries of the school of Monte Cassino and South Italy. On the other hand, they possess some qualities of thought and invention almost in a sublime degree. But I believe Selvo had better work done under him than these. Better work at all events, you shall now see—if you will. You must get hold of the man who keeps sweeping the dust about, in St. Mark's; very thankful he will be, for a lira, to take you up to the gallery on the right-hand side, (south, of St. Mark's interior;) from which gallery, where it turns into the south transept, you may see, as well as it is possible to see, the mosaic of the central dome.

21. Christ enthroned on a rainbow, in a sphere supported by four flying angels underneath, forming white pillars of caryatid mosaic. Between the windows, the twelve apostles, and the Madonna,—alas, the head of this principal figure frightfully " restored," and I think the greater part of the central subject. Round the circle enclosing Christ is written, " Ye men of Galilee, why stand ye at gaze ? This Son of God, Jesus, so taken from you, departs that He may be the arbiter of the earth : in charge of judgment He comes, *and to give the laws that ought to be.*"

22. Such, you see, the central thought of Venetian wor-

ship. Not that we shall leave the world, but that our
Master will come to it: and such the central hope of
Venetian worship, that He shall come to *judge* the world
indeed; not in a last and destroying judgment, but in an
enduring and saving judgment, in truth and righteousness
and peace. Catholic theology of the purest, lasting at all
events down to the thirteenth century; or as long as the
Byzantines had influence. For these are typical Byzantine conceptions: how far taken up and repeated by
Italian workers, one cannot say; but in their gravity of
purpose, meagre thinness of form, and rigid drapery lines,
to be remembered by you with distinctness as expressing
the first school of design in Venice, comparable in an instant with her last school of design, by merely glancing to
the end of the north transept, where that rich piece of
foliage, full of patriarchs, was designed by Paul Veronese.
And what a divine picture it might have been, if he had
only minded his own business, and let the mosaic workers
mind theirs!—even now it is the only beautiful one of
the late mosaics, and shows a new phase of the genius of
Veronese. All I want you to feel, however, is the difference of temper from the time when people liked the white
pillar-like figures of the dome, to that when they liked
the dark exuberance of those in the transept.

23. But from this coign of vantage you may see much
more. Just opposite you, and above, in the arch crossing
the transept between its cupola and the central dome, are
mosaics of Christ's Temptation, and of his entrance to
Jerusalem. The upper one, of the Temptation, is entirely characteristic of the Byzantine mythic manner of
teaching. On the left, Christ sits in the rocky cave which
has sheltered Him for the forty days of fasting: out of

the rock above issues a spring—meaning that He drank of the waters that spring up to everlasting life, of which whoso drinks shall never thirst; and in His hand is a book—the living **Word** of God, which is His bread. The Devil holds up the stones in his lap.

Next the temptation on the pinnacle of the Temple, symbolic again, wholly, as you see,—in very deed quite impossible: so also that on the mountain, where the treasures of the world are, I think, represented by the glittering fragments on the mountain top. Finally, the falling Devil, cast down head-foremost in the air, and approaching angels in ministering troops, complete the story.

24. And on the whole, these pictures are entirely representative to you of the food which the Venetian mind had in art, down to the day of the Doge Selvo. Those were the kind of images and shadows they lived on: you may think of them what you please, but the historic fact is, beyond all possible debate, that these thin dry bones of art were nourishing meat to the Venetian race: that they grew and throve on that diet, every day spiritually fatter for it, and more comfortably round in human soul:—no illustrated papers to be had, no Academy Exhibition to be seen. If their eyes were to be entertained at all, such must be their lugubrious delectation; pleasure difficult enough to imagine, but real and pure, I doubt not; even passionate. In as quite singularly incomprehensible fidelity of sentiment, my cousin's least baby has fallen in love with a wooden spoon; Paul not more devoted to Virginia. The two are inseparable all about the house, vainly the unimaginative bystanders endeavouring to perceive, for their part, any amiableness in the spoon. But baby thrives in his pacific attachment,—nay,

is under the most perfect moral control, pliant as a reed, under the slightest threat of being parted from his spoon. And I am assured that the crescent Venetian imagination did indeed find pleasantness in these figures; more especially,—which is notable—in the extreme emaciation of them,—a type of beauty kept in their hearts down to the Vivarini days; afterwards rapidly changing to a very opposite ideal indeed.

25. Nor even in its most ascetic power, disturbing these conceptions of what was fitting and fair in their own persons, or as a nation of fishermen. They have left us, happily, a picture of themselves, at their greatest time—unnoticed, so far as I can read, by any of their historians, but left for poor little me to discover—and that by chance —like the inscription on St. James's of the Rialto.

But before going on to see this, look behind you, where you stand, at the mosaic on the west wall of the south transept.

It is not Byzantine, but rude thirteenth-century, and fortunately left, being the representation of an event of some import to Venice, the recovery of the lost body of St. Mark.

You may find the story told, with proudly polished, or loudly impudent, incredulity, in any modern guide-book. I will not pause to speak of it here, nor dwell, yet, on this mosaic, which is clearly later than the story it tells by two hundred years. We will go on to the picture which shows us things as they *were*, in its time.

26. You must go round the transept gallery, and get the door opened into the compartment of the eastern aisle, in which is the organ. And going to the other side of the square stone gallery, and looking back from behind the organ, you will see opposite, on the vault, a mosaic of

upright figures in dresses of blue, green, purple, and white, variously embroidered with gold.

These represent, as you are told by the inscription above them—the Priests, the Clergy, the Doge, and the people of Venice; and are an abstract, at least, or epitome of those personages, as they were, and felt themselves to be, in those days.

I believe, early twelfth-century—late eleventh it might be—later twelfth it may be,—it does not matter: these were the people of Venice in the central time of her unwearied life, her unsacrificed honour, her unabated power, and sacred 'faith. Her Doge wears, not the contracted shell-like cap, but the imperial crown. Her priests and clergy are alike mitred—not with the cloven, but simple, cap, like the conical helmet of a knight. Her people are also her soldiers, and their Captain bears his sword, sheathed in black.

So far as features could be rendered in the rude time, the faces are *all* noble—(one horribly restored figure on the right shows what *ignobleness*, on this large scale, modern brutality and ignorance can reach); for the most part, dark-eyed, but the Doge brown-eyed and fair-haired, the long tresses falling on his shoulders, and his beard braided like that of an Etruscan king.

27. And this is the writing over them.

Pontifices. Clerus. Populus. Dux mente serenus.*

---

* The continuing couplet of monkish Latin,

> " Laudibus atque choris
>   Excipiunt dulce canoris,"

may perhaps have been made worse or less efficient Latin by some mistake in restoration.

The Priests. the Clergy. the People. the Duke, serene of mind.

Most Serene Highnesses of all the after Time and World,—how many of you knew, or know, what this Venice, first to give the title, meant by her Duke's Serenity! and why she trusted it?

The most precious "historical picture" this, to my mind, of any in worldly gallery, or unworldly cloister, east or west; but for the present, all I care for you to learn of it, is that these were the kind of priests, and people, and kings, who wrote this Requiem of St. Mark, of which, now, we will read what more we may.

28. If you go up in front of the organ, you may see, better than from below, the mosaics of the eastern dome.

This part of the church must necessarily have been first completed, because it is over the altar and shrine. In it, the teaching of the Mosaic legend begins, and in a sort ends;—"Christ the King," foretold of Prophets—declared of Evangelists—born of a Virgin in due time!

But to understand the course of legend, you must know what the Greek teachers meant by an Evangelion, as distinct from a Prophecy. Prophecy is here thought of in its narrower sense as the foretelling of a good that is to be.

But an Evangelion is the voice of the Messenger, saying, it is *here*.

And the four mystic Evangelists, under the figures of living creatures, are not types merely of the men that are to bring the Gospel message, but of the power of that message in all Creation—so far as it was, and is, spoken in all living things, and as the Word of God, which is Christ, was present, and not merely prophesied, in the Creatures of His hand.

29. You will find in your Murray, and other illumined writings of the nineteenth century, various explanations given of the meaning of the Lion of St. Mark—derived, they occasionally mention, (nearly as if it had been derived by accident!) from the description of Ezekiel.* Which, perhaps, you may have read once on a time, though even that is doubtful in these blessed days of scientific education;—but, boy or girl, man or woman, of you, not one in a thousand, if one, has ever, I am well assured, asked what was the *use* of Ezekiel's Vision, either to Ezekiel, or to anybody else; any more than I used to think, myself, what St. Mark's was built for.

In case you have not a Bible with you, I must be tedious enough to reprint the essential verses here. ￪

30. " As I was among the Captives by the River of Chebar, the Heavens were opened, and I saw visions of God."

(Fugitive at least,—and all *but* captive,—by the River of the deep stream,—the Venetians perhaps cared yet to hear what he saw.)

"In the fifth year of King Jehoiachin's captivity, the word of the Lord came *expressly* unto Ezekiel the Priest."

(We also—we Venetians—have our Pontifices; we also our King. May we not hear?)

" And I looked, and, behold, a whirlwind came out of the north, and a fire infolding itself. Also in the midst thereof was † the likeness of Four living Creatures.

" And this was the aspect of them; the Likeness of a Man was upon them.

---

* Or, with still more enlightened Scripture research, from "one of the visions of Daniel"! (Sketches, etc., p. 18.)

† What alterations I make are from the Septuagint.

"And every one had four faces, and every one four wings. And they had the hands of a Man under their wings. And their wings were stretched upward, two wings of every one were joined one to another, and two covered their bodies. And when they went, I heard the noise of their wings, like the noise of great waters, as the voice of the Almighty, the voice of speech, the noise of an Host."

(To us in Venice, is not the noise of the great waters known—and the noise of an Host? May we hear also the voice of the Almighty?)

"And they went every one straight forward. Whither the Spirit was to go, they went. And this was the likeness of their faces: they four had the face of a Man" (to the front), "and the face of a Lion on the right side, and the face of an Ox on the left side, and" (looking back) "the face of an Eagle."

And not of an Ape, then, my beautifully-browed cockney friend?—the unscientific Prophet! The face of Man; and of the wild beasts of the earth, and of the tame, and of the birds of the air. This was the Vision of the Glory of the Lord.

31. "And as I beheld the living creatures, behold, *one* wheel upon the earth, by the living creatures, with *his* four faces, . . . and their aspect, and their work, was as a wheel in the midst of a wheel."

Crossed, that is, the meridians of the four quarters of the earth. (See Holbein's drawing of it in his Old Testament series.)

"And the likeness of the Firmament upon the heads of the living creatures was as the colour of the terrible crystal.

"And there was a voice from the Firmament that was

over their heads, when they stood, *and had **let down*** their wings.

"**And** above the Firmament that was over their heads **was the** likeness of a Throne; **and upon the** likeness of the Throne was the **likeness** of the Aspect of a Man above, upon it.

"And from His loins round about I saw as **it** were the appearance of fire; and it had brightness round about, as the bow that is in the cloud in the day of rain. This was the appearance of the likeness of the Glory of the Lord. And when **I** saw it, I fell upon **my** face."

32. Can any **of** us do the like—or is it worth while?— with only apes' faces to fall upon, and the forehead that refuses to be ashamed? Or is there, nowadays, no more anything for *us* to be afraid **of, or to** be thankful for, **in** all the wheels, and flame, and light, **of** earth and heaven?

This that follows, **after the** long rebuke, **is their** Evangelion. This the sum of the **voice** that **speaks in** them, (chap. xi. **16**).

"Therefore say, Thus saith **the Lord.** **Though I** have cast them **far** off among **the** heathen, yet will I be to them as a little sanctuary in the places whither they shall come.

"And I will give them one **heart; and** I will put a new spirit within them; and I will take the stony heart out **of** their flesh, and will give them a heart of flesh. That they may walk in my statutes, and keep mine ordinances and do **them,** and they shall be my people, and I will be their God.

"Then did the Cherubims **lift** up their wings, and the wheels beside them, and the glory of the God of Israel was over them above."

5

33. That is the story of the Altar-Vault of St. Mark's, of which though much was gone, yet, when I was last in Venice, much was left, wholly lovely and mighty. The principal figure of the Throned Christ was indeed for ever destroyed by the restorer; but the surrounding Prophets, and the Virgin in prayer, at least retained so much of their ancient colour and expression as to be entirely noble, —if only one had nobility enough in one's own thoughts to forgive the failure of any other human soul to speak clearly what it had felt of most divine.

My notes have got confused, and many lost; and now I have no time to mend the thread of them: I am not sure even if I have the list of the Prophets complete; but these following at least you will find, and (perhaps with others between) in this order—chosen, each, for his message concerning Christ, which is written on the scroll he bears.

34.

1. On the Madonna's left hand, Isaiah. " Behold, a virgin shall conceive." (Written as far as " Immanuel.")

2. Jeremiah. " Hic est in quo,—Deus Noster."

3. Daniel. " Cum venerit " as far as to " cessabit unctio."

4. Obadiah. " Ascendit sanctus in Monte Syon."

5. Habakkuk. " God shall come from the South, and the Holy One from Mount Paran."

6. Hosea. (Undeciphered.)

7. Jonah. (Undeciphered.)

8. Zephaniah. " Seek ye the Lord, all in the gentle time" (in mansueti tempore).

9. Haggai. " Behold, the desired of all nations shall come."

10. Zachariah. "Behold a man whose name is the Branch." (*Oriens.*)

11. Malachi. "Behold, I send my messenger," etc. (angelum meum).

12. Solomon. "Who is this that ascends as the morning?"

13. David. "Of the fruit of thy body will I set upon thy throne."

35. The decorative power of the colour in these figures, chiefly blue, purple, and white, on gold, is entirely admirable,—more especially the dark purple of the Virgin's robe, with lines of gold for its folds; and the figures of David and Solomon, both in Persian tiaras, almost Arab, with falling lappets to the shoulder, for shade; David holding a book with Hebrew letters on it and a cross, (a pretty sign for the Psalms;) and Solomon with rich orbs of lace like involved ornament on his dark robe, ensped in the short hem of it, over gold underneath. And note in all these mosaics that Byzantine "purple,"—the colour at once meaning Kinghood and its Sorrow,—is the same as ours—not scarlet, but amethyst, and that deep.

36. Then in the spandrils below, come the figures of the forr beasts, with this inscription round, for all of them.

> "QUAEQUE SUB OBSCURIS
> DE CRISTO DICTA FIGURIS
> HIS APERIRE DATUR
> ET IN HIS, DEUS IPSE NOTATUR."

"Whatever things under obscure figures have been said of Christ, it is given to *these*" (creatures) "to open; and in these, Christ himself is seen."

A grave saying. Not in the least true of mere Matthew, Mark, Luke, and John. Christ was never seen *in* them, though told of by them. But, as the Word by which all things were made, He is seen in all things made, and in the Poiesis of them : and therefore, when the vision of Ezekiel is repeated to St. John, changed only in that the four creatures are to him more distinct—each with its single aspect, and not each fourfold,—they are full of eyes within, and rest not day nor night,—saying, Holy, Holy, Holy, Lord God Almighty, which art, and wast, and art to come."

37. We repeat the words habitually, in our own most solemn religious service ; but we repeat without noticing out of whose mouths they come.

"Therefore," (we say, in much self-satisfaction,) " with Angels and Archangels, and with all the Company of heaven," (meaning each of us, I suppose, the select Company we expect to get into there,) "we laud and magnify," etc. - But it ought to make a difference in our estimate of ourselves, and of our power to say, with our hearts, that God is Holy, if we remember that we join in saying so, not, for the present, with the Angels,—but with the Beasts.

38. Yet not with every manner of Beast ; for afterwards, when all the Creatures in Heaven and Earth, and the Sea, join in the giving of praise, it is only these four who can say " Amen."

The Ox that treadeth out the corn ; and the Lion that shall eat straw like the Ox, and lie down with the lamb ; and the Eagle that fluttereth over her young ; and the human creature that loves its mate, and its children. In these four is all the power and all the charity of earthly life ; and in such power and charity " Deus ipse notatur."

39. Notable, in that manner, He was, at least, to the men who built this shrine where once was St. Theodore's ; —not betraying nor forgetting their first master, but placing his statue, with St. Mark's Lion, as equal powers upon their pillars of justice;—St. Theodore, as you have before heard, being the human spirit in true conquest over the inhuman, because in true sympathy with it—not as St. George in contest with, but being strengthened and pedestalled by, the " Dragons and all Deeps."

40. But the issue of all these lessons we cannot yet measure ; it is only now that we are beginning to be able to read them, in the myths of the past, and natural history of the present world. The animal gods of Egypt and Assyria, the animal cry that there is *no* God, of the passing hour, are, both of them, part of the rudiments of the religion yet to be revealed, in the rule of the Holy Spirit over the venomous dust, when the sucking child shall play by the hole of the asp, and the weaned child lay his hand on the cockatrice den.

41. And now, if you have enough seen, and understood, this eastern dome and its lesson, go down into the church under the central one, and consider the story of that.

Under *its* angles are the four Evangelists themselves, drawn as men, and each with his name. And over *them* the inscription is widely different.*

* I give, and construe, this legend as now written, but the five letters " liter " are recently restored, and I suspect them to have been originally either three or six, " cer " or " discer." In all the monkish rhymes I have yet read, I don't remember any so awkward a division as this of natura-liter.

" Sic actus Christi
    Describunt quatuor ISTI
    Quod neque natura
    Liter nent, nec utrinque figura."

"Thus do these four describe the Acts of Christ. **And** weave his story, neither by natural knowledge, **nor**, contrariwise, by any figure."

Compare now the two inscriptions. **In the living** creatures, Christ himself is seen by nature and by figure. But these **four** tell us his Acts, "Not by nature—not by figure." How then?

42. You have had **various** "**lives of Christ**," German and **other**, lately provided **among your** other severely historical studies. Some, **critical**; and some, sentimental. But there is only **one** light **by which you can** read the life of Christ,—the light of the life you now lead **in** the flesh; and that not the natural, but the **won life**. "Nevertheless, I live; yet not I, but Christ liveth in me."

Therefore, round the vault, **as** the pillars of it, are the Christian virtues; somewhat **more** in number, and other in nature, than the swindling-born and business-bred virtues which most Christians nowadays are content in acquiring. But these old Venetian virtues are compliant also, in a way. They are for sea-life, and there is one for every wind that blows.

43. If you stand in mid-nave, **looking** to the altar, the first **narrow window** of the cupola—(I call it first for reasons presently given) faces you, in the due east. Call the one next it, **on your** right, the second window; it bears east-south-**east**. The third, south-east; the **fourth, south-south-east;** the **fifth, south;** the ninth,

west; the thirteenth, north; and the sixteenth east-north-east.

The Venetian Virtues stand, one between each window. On the sides of the east window stand Fortitude and Temperance; Temperance the first, Fortitude the last; " he that endureth to the end, the same shall be saved."

Then their **order** is as follows: Temperance between the first and second windows,—(quenching fire with water);—between the second and third, Prudence; and then, in sequence,

    III. Humility.
    IV. Kindness, (Benignitas).
    V. Compassion.
    VI. Abstinence.
    VII. Mercy.
    VIII. Long-suffering.
    IX. Chastity.
    X. Modesty.
    XI. Constancy.
    XII. Charity.
    XIII. Hope.
    XIV. Faith.
    XV. Justice.
    XVI. Fortitude.

44. I meant to have read all their legends, but "could do it any time," and of course never did!—but these following are the most important. Charity is put twelfth at the last attained of the virtues belonging to human life only: but she is called **the** " Mother of the Virtues "— meaning, of them all, when they become divine; and chiefly of **the four** last, which relate to the other world.

Then Long-suffering, (Patientia,) has for her legend, "Blessed are the Peacemakers"; Chastity, "Blessed are the Pure in Heart"; Modesty, "Blessed are ye when men hate you"; while Constancy (consistency) has the two heads, balanced, one in each hand, which are given to the keystone of the entrance arch: meaning, I believe, the equal balance of a man's being, by which it not only stands, but stands as an arch, with the double strength of the two sides of his intellect and soul. "Qui sibi *constat*." Then note that "Modestia" is here not merely shame-facedness, though it includes whatever is good in that; but it is contentment in being thought little of, or hated, when one thinks one ought to be made much of—a very difficult virtue to acquire indeed, as I know some people who know.

45. Then the order of the circle becomes entirely clear. All strength of character begins in temperance, prudence, and lowliness of thought. Without these, nothing is possible, of noble humanity: on these follow—kindness, (simple, as opposed to malice,) and compassion, (sympathy, a much rarer quality than mere kindness); then, self-*restriction*, a quite different and higher condition than temperance,—the first being not painful when rightly practised, but the latter always so;—("I held my peace, even from good "—"quanto quisque sibi plura negaverit, ab Dis plura feret"). Then come pity and long-suffering, which have to deal with the sin, and not merely with the sorrow, of those around us. Then the three Trial virtues, through which one has to struggle forward up to the power of Love, the twelfth.

All these relate only to the duties and relations of the life that is now.

But Love is stronger than Death; and through her, we have, first, Hope of life to come; then, surety of it; living by this surety, (the Just shall live by Faith,) Righteousness, and Strength to the end. Who bears on her scroll, "The Lord shall break the teeth of the Lions."

46. An undeveloped and simial system of human life—you think it—cockney friend!

Such as it was, the Venetians made shift to brave the war of this world with it, as well as ever you are like to do; and they had, besides, the joy of looking to the peace of another. For, you see, above these narrow windows, stand the Apostles, and the two angels that stood by them on the Mount of the Ascension; and between these the Virgin; and with her, and with the twelve, you are to hear the angels' word, "Why stand ye at gaze? as He departs, so shall He come, to give the Laws that ought to be."

DEBITA JURA,

a form of "debit" little referred to in modern ledgers, but by the Venetian acknowledged for all devoirs of commerce and of war; writing, by his church, of the Rialto's business, (the first words, these, mind you, that Venice ever speaks aloud,) "Around this Temple, let the Merchant's law be just, his weights true, and his covenants faithful." And writing thus, in lovelier letters, above the place of St. Mark's Rest,—

> "Brave be the living, who live unto the Lord;
> For Blessed are the dead, that die in Him."

5*

NOTE.—The mosaics described in this number of St. Mark's Rest being now liable at any moment to destruction—from causes already enough specified, I have undertaken, at the instance of Mr. Edward Burne Jones, and with promise of that artist's helpful superintendence, at once to obtain some permanent record of them, the best that may be at present possible : and to that end I have already dispatched to Venice an accomplished young draughtsman, who is content to devote himself, as old painters did, to the work before him for the sake of that, and his own honour, at journeyman's wages. The three of us, Mr. Burne Jones, and he, and I, are alike minded to set our hands and souls hard at this thing : but we can't, unless the public will a little help us. I have given away already all I have to spare, and can't carry on this work at my own cost ; and if Mr. Burne Jones gives his time and care gratis, and without stint, as I know he will, it is all he should be asked for. Therefore, the public must give me enough to maintain my draughtsman at his task : what mode of publication for the drawings may be then possible, is for after-consideration. I ask for subscriptions at present to obtain the copies only. The reader is requested to refer also to the final note appended to the new edition of the " Stones of Venice," and to send what subscription he may please to my publisher, Mr. G. Allen, Sunnyside, Orpington, Kent.

* See appendix to chapter viii., page 187.

FIRST SUPPLEMENT.

THE SHRINE OF THE SLAVES.

BEING A GUIDE TO THE PRINCIPAL PICTURES BY

VICTOR CARPACCIO

IN VENICE.

PREFACE.

THE following (too imperfect) account of the pictures by Carpaccio in the chapel of San Giorgio de' Schiavoni, is properly a supplement to the part of "St. Mark's Rest" in which I propose to examine the religious mind of Venice in the fifteenth century: but I publish these notes prematurely that they may the sooner become helpful, according to their power, to the English traveller.

The second supplement, which is already in the press, will contain the analysis by my fellow-worker, Mr. James Reddie Anderson, of the mythological purport of the pictures here described. I separate Mr. Anderson's work thus distinctly from my own, that he may have the entire credit of it; but the reader will soon perceive that it is altogether necessary, both for the completion and the proof of my tentative statements; and that without the certificate of his scholarly investigation, it would have been lost time to prolong the account of my own conjectures or impressions.

THE SHRINE OF THE SLAVES.

Counting the canals which, entering the city from the open lagoon, must be crossed as you walk from the Piazzetta towards the Public Gardens, the fourth, called the "Rio della Pietà" from the unfinished church of the Pietà, facing the quay before you reach it, will presently, if you go down it in gondola, and pass the Campo di S. Antonin, permit your landing at some steps on the right, in front of a little chapel of indescribable architecture, chiefly made up of foolish spiral flourishes, which yet, by their careful execution and shallow mouldings, are seen to belong to a time of refined temper. Over its door are two bas-reliefs. That of St. Catherine leaning on her wheel seems to me anterior in date to the other, and is very lovely: the second is contemporary with the cinque-cento building, and fine also; but notable chiefly for the conception of the dragon as a creature formidable rather by its gluttony than its malice, and degraded beneath the level of all other spirits of prey; its wings having wasted away into mere paddles or flappers, having in them no faculty or memory of flight; its throat stretched into the flaccidity of a sack, its tail swollen into a molluscous encumbrance, like an enormous worm; and the human head beneath its paw symbolizing therefore the subjection of the human nature to the most brutal desires.

When I came to Venice last year, it was with resolute purpose of finding out everything that could be known of the circumstances which led to the building, and determined the style, of this chapel—or more strictly, sacred hall, of the School of the Schiavoni. But day after day the task was delayed by some more pressing subject of enquiry; and, at this moment—resolved at last to put what notes I have on the contents of it at once together, —I find myself reduced to copy, without any additional illustration, the statement of Flaminio Corner.*

"In the year 1451, some charitable men of the Illyrian or Sclavonic nation, many of whom were sailors, moved by praiseworthy compassion, in that they saw many of their fellow-countrymen, though deserving well of the republic, perish miserably, either of hard life or hunger, nor have enough to pay the expenses of church burial, determined to establish a charitable brotherhood under the invocation of the holy martyrs St. George and St. Trifon— brotherhood whose pledge was to succour poor sailors, and others of their nation, in their grave need, whether by reason of sickness or old age, and to conduct their bodies, after death, religiously to burial. Which design was approved by the Council of Ten, in a decree dated 19th May, 1451; after which, they obtained from the pity of the Prior of the Monastery of St. John of Jerusalem, Lorenzo Marcello, the convenience of a hospice in the buildings of the Priory, with rooms such as were needful for their meetings; and the privilege of building an altar in the

---

* "Notizie Storiche," Venice, 1758, p. 167.

church, under the title of St. George and Trifon, the martyrs ; with the adjudgment of an annual rent of four zec-
chins, two loaves, and a pound of wax, to be offered to the
Priory on the feast of St. George. Such were the begin-
nings of the brotherhood, called that of St. George of the
Sclavonians.

"Towards the close of the fifteenth century, the old
hospice being ruinous, the fraternity took counsel to raise
from the foundations a more splendid new one, under the
title of the Martyr St. George, which was brought to completion, with its façade of marble, in the year 1501."

The hospice granted by the pity of the Prior of St.
John cannot have been very magnificent, if this little
chapel be indeed much more splendid ; nor do I yet know
what rank the school of the Sclavonians held, in power or
number, among the other minor fraternities of Venice.
The relation of the national character of the Dalmatians
and Illyrians, not only to Venice, but to Europe, I find to
be of far more deep and curious interest than is commonly
supposed ; and in the case of the Venetians, traceable
back at least to the days of Herodotus ; for the festival of
the Brides of Venice, and its interruption by the Illyrian
pirates, is one of the curious proofs of the grounds he had
for naming the Venetians as one of the tribes of the Illyrians, and ascribing to them, alone among European races,
the same practice as that of the Babylonians with respect
to the dowries of their marriageable girls.

How it chanced that while the entire Riva,—the chief
quay in Venice—was named from the Sclavonians, they
were yet obliged to build their school on this narrow
canal, and prided themselves on the magnificence of so
small a building, I have not ascertained, nor who the

builder was ;—his style, differing considerably from all the Venetian practice of the same date, by its refusal at once of purely classic forms, and of elaborate ornament, becoming insipidly grotesque, and chastely barbarous, in a quite unexampled degree, is noticeable enough, if we had not better things to notice within the unpretending doorway. Entering, we find ourselves in a little room about the size of the commercial parlour in an old-fashioned English inn; perhaps an inch or two higher in the ceiling, which is of good horizontal beams, narrow and many, for effect of richness; painted and gilded, also, now tawdrily enough, but always in some such patterns as you see. At the end of the low room, is an altar, with doors on the right and left of it in the sides of the room, opening, the one into the sacristy, the other to the stairs leading to the upper chapel. All the rest mere flat wall, wainscoted two-thirds up, eight feet or so, leaving a third of the height, say four feet, claiming some kind of decent decoration. Which modest demand you perceive to be modestly supplied, by pictures, fitting that measure in height, and running long or short, as suits their subjects; ten altogether, (or with the altar-piece, eleven,) of which nine are worth your looking at.

Not as very successfully decorative work, I admit. A modern Parisian upholsterer, or clever Kensington student, would have done for you a far surpassing splendour in a few hours: all that we can say here, at the utmost, is that the place looks comfortable; and, especially, warm,—the pictures having the effect, you will feel presently, of a soft evening sunshine on the walls, or glow from embers on some peaceful hearth, cast up into the room where one sits waiting for dear friends, in twilight.

In a little while, if you still look with general glance, yet patiently, this warmth will **resolve itself** into a kind of chequering, as of an Eastern carpet, **or** old-fashioned English sampler, of more than usually broken and sudden variegation; nay, suggestive here and there of a wayward patchwork, verging into grotesqueness, **or** even, with some touch of fantasy in masque, into harlequinade,—like a tapestry for a Christmas night in a home a thousand years old, to adorn a carol of honoured knights with honouring queens.

Thus far **sentient** of the piece, for all is indeed here but one,—go forward a little, please, to the second picture **on the** left, wherein, central, is our now accustomed friend, **St.** George: stiff and grotesque, even to humorousness, **you** will most likely think him, with his dragon in a singularly depressed and, as it were, water-logged, state. Never mind him, or the dragon, just now ; but take a good opera-glass, and look therewith steadily and long at the heads of **the** two princely riders on the left—the Saracen king and his daughter—he in high white turban, she beyond him in the crimson cap, high, like a castle tower.

Look well and long. For truly,—and with hard-earned and secure knowledge of such matters, I tell you, through all this round world of ours, searching what the best life of it has done of brightest in all its times and years,—you shall not find another piece quite the like of that little piece of work, for supreme, serene, unassuming, unfaltering sweetness of painter's perfect art. Over every other precious thing, of such things known to me, it rises, in the compass of its simplicity ; in being able to gather the perfections of the joy of extreme childhood, and the joy of a hermit's age, with the strength and sunshine of mid-life, all in one.

Which is indeed more or less true of all Carpaccio's work and mind ; but in this piece you have it set in close jewellery, radiant, inestimable.

Extreme joy of childhood, I say. No little lady in her first red shoes,—no soldier's baby seeing himself in the glass beneath his father's helmet, is happier in laugh than Carpaccio, as he heaps and heaps his Sultan's snowy crest, and crowns his pretty lady with her ruby tower. No desert hermit is more temperate ; no ambassador on perilous policy more subtle ; no preacher of first Christian gospel to a primitive race more earnest or tender. The wonderfullest of Venetian Harlequins this,—variegated, like Geryon, to the innermost mind of him—to the lightest gleam of his pencil : " Con piū color, sommesse e sopra-poste ; non fur mai drappi Tartari ne Turchi ; " and all for good.

Of course you will not believe me at first,—nor indeed, till you have unwoven many a fibre of his silk and gold. I had no idea of the make of it myself, till this last year, when I happily had beguiled to Venice one of my best young Oxford men, eager as myself to understand this historic tapestry, and finer fingered than I, who once getting hold of the fringes of it, has followed them thread by thread through all the gleaming damask, and read it clear ; whose account of the real meaning of all these pictures you shall have presently in full.

But first, we will go round the room to know what is here to read, and take inventory of our treasures ; and I will tell you only the little I made out myself, which is all that, without more hard work than can be got through to-day, you are likely either to see in them, or believe of them.

First, on the left, then, St. George and the Dragon— combatant both, to the best of their powers; perfect each in their natures of dragon and knight. No dragon that I know of, pictured among mortal worms; no knight I know of, pictured in immortal chivalry, so perfect, each in his kind, as these two. What else is visible on the battle-ground, of living creature,—frog, newt, or viper,—no less admirable in their kind. The small black viper, central, I have painted carefully for the schools of Oxford as a Natural History study, such as Oxford schools prefer. St. George, for my own satisfaction, also as well as I could, in the year 1872; and hope to get him some day better done, for an example to Sheffield in iron-armour, and several other things.

Picture second, the one I first took you to see, is of the Dragon led into the market-place of the Sultan's capital —submissive: the piece of St. George's spear, which has gone through the back of his head, being used as a bridle: but the creature indeed now little needing one, being otherwise subdued enough; an entirely collapsed and confounded dragon, all his bones dissolved away; prince and people gazing as he returns to his dust.

Picture third, on the left side of the altar.*

The Sultan and his daughter are baptized by St. George.

Triumphant festival of baptism, as at the new birthday of two kingly spirits. Trumpets and shawms high in re-sounding transport; yet something of comic no less than rapturous in the piece; a beautiful scarlet—"parrot"

---

* The intermediate oblong on the lateral wall is not Carpaccio's, and is good for nothing.

(must we call him?) conspicuously mumbling at a violet flower under the steps; him also—finding him the scarletest and mumblingest parrot I had ever seen—I tried to paint in 1872 for the Natural History Schools of Oxford—perhaps a new species, or extinct old one, to immortalize Carpaccio's name and mine. When all the imaginative arts shall be known no more, perhaps, in Darwinian Museum, this scarlet "Epops Carpaccii" may preserve our fame.

But the quaintest thing of all is St. George's own attitude in baptizing. He has taken a good platterful of water to pour on the Sultan's head. The font of inlaid bronze below is quite flat, and the splash is likely to be spreading. St. George—carefullest of saints, it seems, in the smallest matters—is holding his mantle back well out of the way. I suppose, really and truly, the instinctive action would have been this, pouring at the same time so that the splash might be towards himself, and not over the Sultan.

With its head close to St. George's foot, you see a sharp-eared white dog, with a red collar round his neck. Not a greyhound, by any means; but an awkward animal; stupid-looking, and not much like a saint's dog. Nor is it in the least interested in the baptism, which a saint's dog would certainly have been. The mumbling parrot, and he—what *can* they have to do with the proceedings? A very comic picture!

But this next,—for a piece of sacred art, what can we say of it?

St. Tryphonius and the Basilisk—was ever so simple a saint, ever so absurd a beast? as if the absurdity of all heraldic beasts that ever were, had been hatched into one perfect absurdity—prancing there on the steps of the

throne, self-satisfied ;—*this* the beast whose glance is
mortal!   And little St. Tryphonius, with nothing remarkable about him more than is in every good little boy, for
all I can see.

And the worst of it is that I don't happen to know
anything about St. Tryphonius, whom I mix up a little
with Trophonius, and his **cave ; also I** am not very
clear about the difference between basilisks and cocka-
trices; and on the whole find myself reduced, in this
picture, to admiring the carpets with the crosses on them
hung out of the window, which, if you will examine with
opera-glass, you **will be** convinced, I think, that nobody
can do the like of them by rules, at Kensington ; and that
if you really care to have carpets as good as they can be,
you must get somebody to design them who can draw
saints and basilisks too.

Note, also, the group under the loggia which the stair-
case leads up to, high on the left.   It is a picture in itself;
far more lovely as a composition than the finest Titian or
Veronese, simple **and** pleasant this as the summer air, and
lucent as morning cloud.

On the other side also there are wonderful things, only
there's a black figure there that frightens me ; I can't
make it out at all; and would rather go on to the next
picture, please.

Stay—I forgot the arabesque on the steps, with the
living plants taking part in the ornament, like voices
chanting here and there a note, as some pretty tune follows
its melodious way, on constant instruments.   Nature and
art at play with each other—graceful and gay alike, yet
all the while conscious that they are at play round the
steps of a throne, and under the paws of a basilisk.

The fifth picture is in the darkest recess of all the room ; and of darkest theme,—the Agony in the garden. I have never seen it rightly, nor need you pause at it, unless to note the extreme naturalness of the action in the sleeping figures—their dresses drawn tight under them as they have turned, restlessly. But the principal figure is hopelessly invisible.

The sixth picture is of the calling of Matthew ; visible, this, in a bright day, and worth waiting for one, to see it in, through any stress of weather.

For, indeed, the Gospel which the publican wrote for us, with its perfect Sermon on the Mount, and mostly more harmonious and gentle fulness, in places where St. Luke is formal, St. John mysterious, and St. Mark brief,—this Gospel, according to St. Matthew, I should think, if we had to choose one ont of all the books in the Bible for a prison or desert friend, would be the one we should keep.

And we do not enough think how much that leaving the receipt of custom meant, as a sign of the man's nature, who was to leave us such a notable piece of literature.

Yet observe, Carpaccio does not mean to express the fact, or anything like the fact, of the literal calling of Matthew. What the actual character of the publicans of Jerusalem was at that time, in its general aspect, its admitted degradation, and yet power of believing, with the harlot, what the masters and the mothers in Israel could not believe, it is not his purpose to teach you. This call from receipt of custom, he takes for the symbol of the universal call to leave all that we have, and are doing. " Whosoever forsaketh not all that he hath, cannot be my disciple." For the other calls were easily obeyed in com-

parison of this. To leave one's often empty nets and
nightly toil on sea, and become fishers of men, probably
you might find pescatori enough on the Riva there, within
a hundred paces of you, who would take the chance at
once, if any gentle person offered it them. James and
Jude—Christ's cousins—no thanks to them for following
Him; their own home conceivably no richer than His.
Thomas and Philip, I suppose, somewhat thoughtful persons on spiritual matters, questioning of them long since;
going out to hear St. John preach, and to see whom he
had seen. But *this* man, busy in the place of business—
engaged in the interests of foreign governments—thinking
no more of an Israelite Messiah than Mr. Goschen, but
only of Egyptian finance, and the like—suddenly the
Messiah, passing by, says "Follow me!" and he rises up,
gives Him his hand, "Yea! to the death;" and absconds
from his desk in that electric manner on the instant,
leaving his cash-box unlocked, and his books for whoso
list to balance!—a very remarkable kind of person indeed,
it seems to me.

Carpaccio takes him, as I said, for a type of such sacrifice at its best. Everything (observe in passing) is here
given you of the best. Dragon deadliest—knight purest
—parrot scarletest—basilisk absurdest—publican publi-
canest;—a perfect type of the life spent in taxing one's
neighbour, exacting duties, per-centages, profits in general,
in a due and virtuous manner.

For do not think Christ would have called a bad or
corrupt publican—much less that a bad or corrupt publican would have obeyed the call. Your modern English
evangelical doctrine that Christ has a special liking for
the souls of rascals is the absurdest basilisk of a doctrine

6

that ever pranced on judgment steps. That which is *lost*
He comes to save,—yes; but not that which is defiantly
going the way He has forbidden. He showed you plainly
enough what kind of publican He would call, having
chosen two, both of the best: "Behold, Lord, if I have
taken anything from any man, I restore it fourfold!"—a
beautiful manner of trade. Carpaccio knows well that
there were no defalcations from Levi's chest—no oppres-
sions in his tax-gathering. This whom he has painted is
a true merchant of Venice, uprightest and gentlest of the
merchant race; yet with a glorious pride in him. What
merchant but one of Venice would have ventured to take
Christ's hand, as his friend's—as one man takes another's? Not repentant, he, of anything he has done;
not crushed or terrified by Christ's call; but rejoicing in
it, as meaning Christ's praise and love. "Come up higher
then, for there are nobler treasures than these to count,
and a nobler King than this to render account to. Thou
hast been faithful over a few things; enter thou into the
joy of thy Lord."

A lovely picture, in every sense and power of painting;
natural, and graceful, and quiet, and pathetic;—divinely
religious, yet as decorative and dainty as a bank of violets
in spring.

But the next picture! How was ever such a thing
allowed to be put in a church? Nothing surely could be
more perfect in comic art. St. Jerome, forsooth, intro-
ducing his novice lion to monastic life, with the resulting
effect on the vulgar monastic mind.

Do not imagine for an instant that Carpaccio does not
see the jest in all this, as well as you do,—perhaps even a
little better. "Ask for him to-morrow, indeed, and you

shall find him a grave man;" but, to-day, Mercutio himself is not more fanciful, nor Shakespeare himself more
gay in his fancy of "the gentle beast and of a good conscience," than here the painter as he drew his delicately
smiling lion with his head on one side like a Perugino's
saint, and his left paw raised, partly to show the thorn
wound, partly in deprecation,—

> " For if I should, as lion, come in strife
> Into this place, 'twere pity of my life.

The flying monks are scarcely at first intelligible but as
white and blue oblique masses; and there was much
debate between Mr. Murray and me, as he sketched the
picture for the Sheffield Museum, whether the actions of
flight were indeed well given or not; he maintaining that
the monks were really running like Olympic archers, and
that the fine drawing was only lost under the quartering
of the dresses;—I on the contrary believe that Carpaccio
had failed, having no gift for representing swift motion.
We are probably both right; I doubt not that the running
action, if Mr. Murray says so, is rightly drawn; but at
this time, every Venetian painter had been trained to
represent only slow and dignified motion, and not till
fifty years later, under classic influence, came the floating
and rushing force of Veronese and Tintoret.

And I am confirmed in this impression by the figure of
the stag in the distance, which does not run freely, and
by the imperfect gallop of St. George's horse in the first
subject.

But there are many deeper questions respecting this
St. Jerome subject than those of artistic skill. The picture
is a jest indeed; but is it a jest only? Is the tradition

itself a jest? or only by our own fault, and perhaps Carpaccio's, do we make it so?

. In the first place, then, you will please to remember, as
I have often told you, Carpaccio is not answerable for
himself in this matter. He begins to think of his subject,
intending, doubtless, to execute it quite seriously. But
his mind no sooner fastens on it than the vision of it
comes to him as a jest, and he is forced to paint it.
Forced by the fates,—dealing with the fate of Venice and
Christendom. We must ask of Atropos, not of Carpaccio,
why this picture makes us laugh; and why the tradition
it records has become to us a dream and a scorn. No day
of my life passes now to its sunset, without leaving me
more doubtful of all our cherished contempts, and more
earnest to discover what root there was for the stories of
good men, which are now the mocker's treasure.

And I want to read a good "Life of St. Jerome." And
if I go to Mr. Ongaria's I shall find, I suppose, the auto-
biography of George Sand, and the life of—Mr. Sterling,
perhaps; and Mr. Werner, written by my own master,
and which indeed I've read, but forget now who either
Mr. Sterling or Mr. Werner were; and perhaps, in religious literature, the life of Mr. Wilberforce and of Mrs.
Fry; but not the smallest scrap of information about St.
Jerome. To whom, nevertheless, all the charity of George
Sand, and all the ingenuity of Mr. Sterling, and all the
benevolence of Mr. Wilberforce, and a great quantity, if
we knew it, of the daily comfort and peace of our own
little lives every day, are verily owing; as to a lovely old
pair of spiritual spectacles, without whom we never had
read a word of the "Protestant Bible." It is of no use,
however, to begin a life of St. Jerome now—and of little

use to look at these pictures without a life of St. Jerome;
but only thus much you should be clear in knowing about
him, as not in the least doubtful or mythical, but wholly
true, and the beginning of facts quite limitlessly important
to all modern Europe—namely, that he was born of good,
or at least rich family, in Dalmatia, virtually midway between the east and the west; that he made the great
Eastern book, the Bible, legible in the west; that he was
the first great teacher of the nobleness of ascetic scholarship and courtesy, as opposed to ascetic savageness :—the
founder, properly, of the ordered cell and tended garden,
where before was but the desert and the wild wood; and
that he died in the monastery he had founded at Bethlehem.

It is this union of gentleness and refinement with noble
continence,—this love and imagination illuminating the
mountain cave into a frescoed cloister, and winning its
savage beasts into domestic friends, which Carpaccio has
been ordered to paint for you; which, with ceaseless
exquisiteness of fancy, he fills these three canvases with
the incidents of,—meaning, as I believe, the story of all
monastic life, and death, and spiritual life for evermore :
the power of this great and wise and kind spirit, ruling in
the perpetual future over all household scholarship; and
the help rendered by the companion souls of the lower
creatures to the highest intellect and virtue of man.

And if with the last picture of St. Jerome in his study,
—his happy white dog watching his face—you will men-
tally compare a hunting piece by Rubens, or Snyders,
with the torn dogs rolled along the ground in their blood,
—you may perhaps begin to feel that there is something
more serious in this kaleidoscope of St. George's Chapel

than you at first believed—which if you now care to follow out with me, let us think over this ludicrous subject
more quietly.   .

What account have we here given, voluntarily or invol-
untarily, of monastic life, by a man of the keenest perception, living in the midst of it? That all the monks
who have caught sight of the lion should be terrified out
of their wits—what a curious witness to the *timidity* of
Monasticism! Here are people professing to prefer
Heaven to earth—preparing themselves for the change as
the reward of all their present self-denial. And this is
the way they receive the first chance of it that offers!

Evidently Carpaccio's impression of monks must be, not
that they were more brave or good than other men ; but
that they liked books, and gardens, and peace, and were
afraid of death—therefore, retiring from the warrior's
danger of chivalry somewhat selfishly and meanly. He
clearly takes the knight's view of them. What he may
afterwards tell us of good concerning them, will not be
from a witness prejudiced in their favour. Some good
he tells us, however, even here. The pleasant order in
wildness of the trees; the buildings for agricultural and
religious use, set down as if in an American clearing, here
and there, as the ground was got ready for them ; the
perfect grace of cheerful, pure, illuminating art, filling
every little cornice-cusp of the chapel with its jewel-pic-
ture of a saint,*—last, and chiefly, the perfect kindness to
and fondness for, all sorts of animals. Cannot you better
conceive, as you gaze upon the happy scene, what manner
of men they were who first secured from noise of war the

---

* See the piece of distant monastery in the lion picture, with its fragments of fresco on wall, its ivy-covered door, and illuminated cornice.

sweet nooks of meadow beside your own mountain streams at Bolton, and Fountains, Furness and Tintern ? But of the saint himself Carpaccio has all good to tell you. Common monks were, at least, harmless creatures ; but here is a strong and beneficent one. "Calm, before the Lion ! " say C. C. with their usual perspicacity, as if the story were that the saint alone had courage to confront the raging beast—a Daniel in the lions' den ! They might as well say of Carpaccio's Venetian beauty that she is "calm before the lapdog." The saint is leading in his new pet, as he would a lamb, and vainly expostulating with his brethren for being ridiculous. The grass on which they have dropped their books is beset with flowers ; there is no sign of trouble or asceticism on the old man's face, he is evidently altogether happy, his life being complete, and the entire scene one of the ideal simplicity and security of heavenly wisdom : "Her ways are ways of pleasantness, and all her paths are peace."

And now pass to the second picture. At first you will perhaps see principally its weak monks—looking more foolish in their sorrow than ever they did in their fear. Portraits these, evidently, every soul of them—chiefly the one in spectacles, reading the funeral service so perfunctorily,—types, throughout, of the supreme commonplace ; alike in action and expression, except those quiet ones in purple on the right, and the grand old man on crutches, come to see this sight.

But St. Jerome himself in the midst of them, the eager heart of him quiet, to such uttermost quietness,—the body lying—look—absolutely flat like clay, as if it had been beat down, and clung, clogged, all along to the marble. Earth to earth indeed. Level clay and inlaid rock now all one—and the noble head senseless as a stone, with a stone for its pillow.

There they gather **and kneel** about it—wondering, I think, more than pitying. To see what was yesterday the great Life in the midst of them, laid thus! But, so far as they do not wonder, they pity only, and grieve. There is no looking for his soul in the clouds,—no worship of relics here, implied even in the kneeling figures. All **look** down, woefully, wistfully, as into a grave. "And so Death passed upon all men, for that all have sinned."

This is Carpaccio's message to us. And lest you should not read **it, and** carelessly think that he meant only the usual commonplace of the **sacredness and** blessedness of the **death of the righteous,—look into** the narrow shadow in the corner of the house **at the left** hand side, where, on the strange forked and leafless tree that occupies it, are **set** the cross and little vessel of holy water beneath, and above, the skull, which are always the signs of St. Jerome's place of prayer in the desert.

The lower jaw has fallen from the skull *into the vessel of holy water.*

It is but **a** little sign,—but you will soon know how much this painter indicates by such things, and that here he means indeed that for the greatest, as the meanest, of the sons of Adam, death is still the sign of their sin ; and that **though in** Christ all shall be made alive, yet also in Adam **all** die ; and this return **to their** earth is not in itself the coming of peace, but the infliction of shame.

At the lower edge **of** the marble pavement is one of Carpaccio's lovely signatures, on **a white scroll,** held in its **mouth by** a tiny lizard.

And now you will be able to enter into the joy of the last picture, the life of St. Jerome in Heaven.

I had no thought, myself, of this being the meaning of such closing scene; but the evidence for this reading of it, laid before me by my fellow-worker, Mr. Anderson, seems to me, in the concurrence of its many clauses, irresistible; and this at least is certain, that as the opposite St. George represents the perfect Mastery of the body, in contest with the lusts of the Flesh, this of St. Jerome represents the perfect Mastery of the mind, in the fulfilment of the right desires of the Spirit: and all the arts of man,—music (a long passage of melody written clear on one of the fallen scrolls), painting (in the illuminated missal and golden alcove), and sculpture (in all the forms of furniture and the bronze work of scattered ornaments), —these—and the glad fidelity of the lower animals,—all subjected in pleasant service to the more and more perfect reading and teaching of the Word of God;—read, not in written pages chiefly, but with uplifted eyes by the light of Heaven itself, entering and filling the mansions of Immortality.

This interpretation of the picture is made still more probable, by the infinite pains which Carpaccio has given to the working of it. It is quite impossible to find more beautiful and right painting of detail, or more truthful tones of atmosphere and shadow affecting interior colours.

Here then are the principal heads of the symbolic evidence, abstracted for us by Mr. Anderson from his complete account of the whole series, now in preparation.

1. "The position of the picture seems to show that it

6*

sums up the whole matter. The St. George series reads
from left to right. So, chronologically, the two others of
St. Jerome ; but this, which should according to the story
have been first, appears **after the death**.

2. "The figure on the altar **is—most** unusually—our
Lord with the Resurrection-banner. The shadow of this
figure falls on the wall so as **to** make a crest for the mitre
on the altar—'Helmet of Salvation.' . . . . The mitre
(by comparison with St. Ursula's arrival in Rome **it is a**
cardinal's mitre), censer, and crosier, are laid aside.

3. "**The** Communion and Baptismal vessels are also
laid aside under this altar, not of the dead but of the
Risen Lord. The curtain falling from the altar is drawn
aside that we may notice this.

4. " In the mosaic-covered recess above the altar there
is prominently **inlaid the figure of a cherub** or seraph
' che in Dio più l'occhio ha fisso.'

5. "Comparing the colours **of the** winged and four-
footed parts of the ' animal binato ' in the Purgatory, it is
I believe important to notice that the statue of our Lord
is gold, the dress of St. Jerome **red** and white, and over
the shoulders a cape of the **brown** colour of earth.

6. " While candles blaze round the dead Jerome in the
previous picture, the candlesticks on the altar here are
empty—'they need no candle.'

7. " The two round-topped windows in line behind the
square **one** through which **St.** Jerome gazes, are the ancient tables bearing **the** message **of** light, delivered ' of
angels ' to the faithful, but **now put** behind, and comparatively dim beside the glory of present **and** personal vision. **Yet** the light which comes even through the square
window streams through bars like those of a prison.

    " 'Through the body's prison bars
    His soul possessed the sun and stars,'

Dante Rossetti writes of Dante Allighieri; but Carpaccio hangs the wheels of all visible heaven *inside* these bars. **St.** Jerome's ' possessions' are in a farther country. These bars are another way of putting what is signified by the brown cape.

8. " The two great volumes leaning against the wall by the arm-chair are the same thing, the closed testaments.

9. " The **documents** hanging in the little chamber behind and **lying at the** saint's feet, remarkable for their hanging **seals**, are shown by these seals to be titles to some property, **or** testaments; **but** they are now put aside **or** thrown underfoot. Why, except that possession is gotten, that Christ is risen, and that ' a testament is of no strength at all while the testator liveth ' ? This **I** believe is no misuse of Paul's **words, but** an employment of them in their mystic sense, just as **the New** Testament **writers** quoted the **Old** Testament. There is a very prominent illuminated R on one of the documents under the **table** (I think you have **written of it as Greek in its lines**): I cannot but fancy **it is the initial letter of** ' Resurrectio.' What the music **is**, Caird has **sent** me no information about; **he was to** enquire of some friend who knew about old church music. The prominent bell and shell **on the** table puzzle me, but I am sure mean something. Is the former the mass-bell ?

10. " The **statuettes of Venus and** the horse, and the various antique fragments **on** the shelf behind the arm-chair are, I think, symbols **of** the world, of the flesh, **placed** behind even the old Scripture studies. You re-

member Jerome's early learning, and the vision that awakened him from Pagan thoughts (to read the laws of the True City) with the words, ' Ubi est thesaurus tuus.'

"I have put these things down without trying to dress them into an argument, that you may judge them as one would gather them hap-hazard from the picture. Individually several of them might be weak arguments, but together I do think they are conclusive. The key-note is struck by the empty altar bearing the risen Lord. I do not think Carpaccio thought of immortality in the symbols derived from mortal life, through which the ordinary mind feels after it. Nor surely did Dante (V. esp. Par. IV. 27 and following lines). And think of the words in Canto II:—

> " ' Dentro dal ciel della Divina Pace
> Si gira un corpo nella cui virtute
> L'esser di tutto suo contento giace.'

But there is no use heaping up passages, as the sense that in using human language he merely uses mystic metaphor is continually present in Dante, and often explicitly stated. And it is surely the error of regarding these picture writings for children who live in the nursery of Time and Space, as if they were the truth itself, which can be discovered only spiritually, that leads to the inconsistencies of thought and foolish talk of even good men.

" St. Jerome, in this picture, is young and brown-haired, not bent and with long white beard, as in the two others. I connect this with the few who have stretched their necks

> " ' Per tempo al pan degli angeli del quale
> Vivesi qui ma non si vien satollo.'

St. Jerome lives here by what is really the immortal bread;

but shall **not** here be filled with it so as to hunger no
more; and under his earthly cloak comprehends as little
perhaps the Great **Love** he hungers after and is fed by,
as his dog comprehends him. **I** am sure the dog is there
with some such purpose of comparison. **On** that very
last quoted passage **of** Dante, Landino's commentary (it
was printed in Venice, **1491**) **annotates the** words 'che
drizzaste 'l collo,' with a quotation,

> " ' **Cum** spectant animalia cetera terram
> Os homini sublime dedit, coelum tueri jussit.'

I was **myself brought** entirely **to** pause of happy wonder
when first **my friend** showed me the lessons hidden in
these pictures; nor do I at all expect the reader at first to
believe them. But the condition of his possible belief in
them is that he approach them with a pure heart and a
meek one; for this Carpaccio teaching is like the talisman
of Saladin, which, dipped in pure water, made it **a** healing
draught, **but by** itself seemed only a little inwoven web of
silk and gold.

But to-day, that **we** may **be** able **to read** better to-
morrow, we will **leave** this cell of sweet mysteries, and
examine some **of the** painter's earlier work, **in** which we
may learn his way of writing more completely, and understand the degree in which his own personal character, **or**
prejudices, or imperfections, mingle in the method of his
scholarship, and colour or **divert** the current of his inspiration.

Therefore now, taking gondola again, you **must be**
carried through the sea-streets **to a** far-away church, in
the part of Venice now wholly abandoned to the poor,
though a kingly saint's—St. Louis's : but there are other

things in this church to be noted, besides Carpaccio, which will be useful in illustration of him ; and to see these rightly, you must compare with them things of the same kind in another church where there are no Carpaccios,— namely, St. Pantaleone, to which, being the nearer, you had better first direct your gondolier.

For the ceilings alone of these two churches, St. Pantaleone and St. Alvise, are worth a day's pilgrimage in their sorrowful lesson.

All the mischief that Paul Veronese did may be seen in the halting and hollow magnificences of them ;—all the absurdities, either of painting or piety, under afflatus of vile ambition. Roof puffed up and broken through, as it were, with breath of the fiend from below, instead of pierced by heaven's light from above ; the rags and ruins of Venetian skill, honour, and worship, exploded all together sky-high. Miracles of frantic mistake, of flaunting and thunderous hypocrisy,—universal lie, shouted through speaking-trumpets.

If I could let you stand for a few minutes, first under Giotto's four-square vault at Assisi, only thirty feet from the ground, the four triangles of it written with the word of God close as an illuminated missal, and then suddenly take you under these vast staggering Temples of Folly and Iniquity, you would know what to think of "modern development" thenceforth.

The roof of St. Pantaleone is, I suppose, the most curious example in Europe of the vulgar dramatic effects of painting. That of St. Alvise is little more than a caricature of the mean passion for perspective, which was the first effect of "science" joining itself with art. And under it, by strange coincidence, there are also two notable

pieces of plausible modern sentiment,—celebrated pieces
by Tiepolo.   He is virtually the beginner of Modernism:
these two pictures of his are exactly like what a first-rate
Parisian Academy student would do, setting himself to
conceive the sentiment of Christ's flagellation, after having
read unlimited quantities of George Sand and Dumas.
It is well that they chance to be here: look thoroughly at
them and their dramatic chiaroscuros for a little time,
observing that no face is without some expression of crime
or pain, and that everything is always put dark against
light or light against dark.   Then return to the entrance
of the church, where under the gallery, frameless and
neglected, hang eight old pictures,—bought, the story
goes, at a pawnbroker's in the Giudecca for forty sous
each,*—to me among the most interesting pieces of art
in North Italy, for they are the only examples I know of
an entirely great man's work in extreme youth.   They
are Carpaccio's, when he cannot have been more than
eight or ten years old, and painted then half in precocious
pride and half in play.   I would give anything to know
their real history.   "School pictures," C. C. call them!
as if they were merely bad imitations, when they are the
most unaccountable and unexpected pieces of absurd fancy
that ever came into a boy's head, and scrabbled, rather
than painted, by a boy's hand,—yet, with the eternal
master-touch in them already.

SUBJECTS.—1. Rachel at the **Well**. 2. Jacob and his
Sons before Joseph.   3. Tobias and the Angel.   4. The
Three Holy Children.   5. Job.   6. Moses, and Adoration

---

* "Originally in St. Maria della Vergine" (C. C.).   Why are not
the documents on the authority of which these statements are made
given clearly ?

of Golden Calf (C.C.).   7. Solomon and the Queen of
Sheba.   8. Joshua and falling Jericho.

In all these pictures the qualities of Carpaćcio are
already entirely pronounced ; the grace, quaintness, simplicity, and deep intentness on the meaning of incidents.
I don't know if the grim statue in No. 4 is, as C. C. have
it, the statue of Nebuchadnezzar's dream, or that which
he erected for the three holy ones to worship,—and
already I forget how the "worship of the golden calf"
according to C. C., and "Moses" according to my note,
(and I believe the inscription, for most of, if not all, the
subjects are inscribed with the names of the persons
represented,) are relatively pourtrayed.   But I have not
forgotten, and beg my reader to note specially, the exquisite strangeness of the boy's rendering of the meeting
of Solomon and the Queen of Sheba.   One would have
expected the Queen's retinue, and her spice-bearing
camels, and Solomon's house and his servants, and his
cup-bearers in all their glory ; and instead of this, Solomon and the Queen stand at the opposite ends of a little
wooden bridge over a ditch, and there is not another soul
near them,—and the question seems to be which first shall
set foot on it !

Now, what can we expect in the future of the man or
boy who conceives his subjects, or is liable to conceive
them, after this sort?   There is clearly something in his
head which we cannot at all make out; a ditch must be
to him the Rubicon, the Euphrates, the Red Sea,—Heaven
only knows what! a wooden bridge must be Rialto in
embryo.   This unattended King and Queen must mean
the pre-eminence of uncounselled royalty, or what not ;
in a word, there's no saying, and no criticizing him ; and

the less, because his gift of colour and his **enjoyment of all visible things** around him are so intense, **so instinctive, and so constant**, that he **is never to be thought of as a** responsible person, but **only** as a kind of **magic mirror** which flashes back instantly whatever it **sees beautifully** arranged, but yet will flash **back commonplace things** often as faithfully as others.

I was especially struck with this character of his, **as** opposed to the grave and balanced design of Luini, when after working six months with Carpaccio, I went back to the St. **Stephen** at Milan, in the Monasterio Maggiore. In order **to do** justice to either painter, they should be alternately studied for a little while. In one respect, Luini greatly gains, and Carpaccio suffers by this trial; **for** whatever is in the least flat or hard in the Venetian is felt more violently by contrast with the infinite sweetness of the Lombard's harmonies, while only by contrast with the vivacity of the Venetian **can** you entirely feel the depth in faintness, and the grace in quietness, of Luini's chiaroscuro. But the principal point of difference is in the command which Luini has **over his** thoughts, every design of his being concentrated on its main purpose with quite visible art, and all accessories that would in the least have interfered with it withdrawn in merciless asceticism; whereas a subject under Carpaccio's hand is always just as it would or might have occurred in nature; and among a myriad of trivial incidents, you are left, by your own sense and sympathy, to discover the vital one.

For instance, there are two small pictures of his in the Brera gallery at Milan, which may at once be compared with the Luinis there. I find the following notice of them in my **diary** for 6th September, 1876 :—

"Here, in the sweet air, with a whole world in ruin round me. The misery of my walk through the Brera yesterday no tongue can tell; but two curious lessons were given me by Carpaccio. The first, in his preaching of St. Stephen—Stephen up in the corner where nobody would think of him; the doctors, one in lecture throne, the rest in standing groups mostly—Stephen's face radiant with true soul of heaven,—the doctors, not monsters of iniquity at all, but superbly true and quiet studies from the doctors of Carpaccio's time; doctors of this world—not one with that look of heaven, but respectable to the uttermost, able, just, penetrating: a complete assembly of highly trained old Oxford men, but with more intentness. The second, the Virgin going up to the temple; and under the steps of it, a child of ten or twelve with his back to us, dressed in a parti-coloured, square-cut robe, holding a fawn in leash, at his side a rabbit; on the steps under the Virgin's feet a bas-relief of fierce fight of men with horned monsters like rampant snails : one with a conger-eel's body, twining round the limb of the man who strikes it."

Now both these pictures are liable to be passed almost without notice ; they scarcely claim to be compositions at all ; but the one is a confused group of portraits ; the other, a quaint piece of grotesque, apparently without any meaning, the principal feature in it, a child in a parti-coloured cloak. It is only when, with more knowledge of what we may expect from the painter, we examine both pictures carefully, that the real sense of either comes upon us. For the heavenly look on the face of Stephen is not set off with raised light, or opposed shade, or principality of place. The master trusts only to what nature herself would have trusted in—expression pure and simple. If you cannot see heaven in the boy's mind, without any turning on of the stage lights, you shall not see it at all.

There is some one else, however, whom you may see, on looking carefully enough. On the opposite side of the group of old doctors is another youth, just of Stephen's age. And as the face of Stephen is full of heavenly rapture, so that of his opposite is full of darkest wrath,—the religious wrath which all the authority of the conscience urges, instead of quenching. The old doctors hear Stephen's speech with doubtful pause of gloom; but this youth has no patience,—no endurance for it. He will be the first to cry, Away with him,—" Whosoever will cast a stone at him, let them lay their mantle at my feet."

Again—looking again and longer at the other pictures, you will first correct my mistake of writing "fawn "— discovering the creature held by the boy to be a unicorn.* Then you will at once know that the whole must be symbolic; and looking for the meaning of the unicorn, you find it signifies chastity; and then you see that the bas-relief on the steps, which the little Virgin ascends, must mean the warring of the old strengths of the world with lust: which theme you will find presently taken up also and completed by the symbols of St. George's Chapel. If now you pass from these pictures to any of the Luini frescoes in the same gallery, you will at once recognize a total difference in conception and treatment. The thing which Luini wishes you to observe is held forth to you with direct and instant proclamation. The saint, angel, or Madonna, is made central or principal; every figure in the surrounding group is subordinate, and every accessory

* Corrected for me by Mr. C. F. Murray.

subdued or generalized. All the precepts of conventional art are obeyed, and the invention and originality of the master are only shown by the variety with which he adorns the commonplace,—by the unexpected grace with which he executes what all have done,—and the sudden freshness with which he invests what all have thought.

This external difference in the manner of the two painters is connected with a much deeper element in the constitution of their minds. To Carpaccio, whatever he has to represent must be a reality; whether a symbol or not, afterwards, is no matter, the first condition is that it shall be real. A serpent, or a bird, may perhaps mean iniquity or purity; but primarily, they must have real scales and feathers. But with Luini, everything is primarily an idea, and only realized so far as to enable you to understand what is meant. When St. Stephen stands beside Christ at his scourging, and turns to us who look on, asking with unmistakable passion, "Was ever sorrow like this sorrow?" Luini does not mean that St. Stephen really stood there; but only that the thought of the saint who first saw Christ in glory may best lead us to the thought of Christ in pain. But when Carpaccio paints St. Stephen preaching, he means to make us believe that St. Stephen really did preach, and as far as he can, to show us exactly how he did it.

And, lastly, to return to the point at which we left him. His own notion of the way things happened may be a very curious one, and the more so that it cannot be regulated even by himself, but is the result of the singular power he has of seeing things in vision as if they were real. So that when, as we have seen, he paints Solomon and the Queen of Sheba standing at opposite ends of a wooden bridge over a ditch, we are not to suppose the two persons are less real to him on that account, though absurd to us; but we are to understand that such a vision of them did indeed appear to the boy who had passed all his dawning life among wooden bridges, over ditches; and had the habit besides of spiritualizing, or reading like a vision, whatever he saw with eyes either of the body or mind.

The delight which he had in this faculty of vision, and the industry with which he cultivated it, can only be justly estimated by close examination of the marvellous picture in the Correr Museum, representing two Venetian ladies with their pets.

In the last general statement I have made of the rank of painters, I named two pictures of John Bellini, the Madonna in San Zaccaria, and that in the sacristy of the Frari, as, so far as my knowledge went, the two best pictures in the world. In that estimate of them I of course considered as one chief element, their solemnity of purpose—as another, their unpretending simplicity. Putting aside these higher conditions, and looking only to perfection of execution and essentially artistic power of design, I rank this Carpaccio above either of them, and therefore, as in these respects, the best picture in the world. I know no other which unites every nameable quality of painter's art in so intense a degree—breadth with minuteness, brilliancy with quietness, decision with tenderness, colour with light and shade: all that is faithfullest in Holland, fancifullest in Venice, severest in Florence, naturalest in England. Whatever de Hooghe could do in shade, Van Eyck in detail—Giorgione in mass—Titian in colour—Bewick and Landseer in animal life, is here at once ; and I know no other picture in the world which can be compared with it.

It is in tempera, however, not oil : and I must note in passing that many of the qualities which I have been in the habit of praising in Tintoret and Carpaccio, as consummate achievements in oil-painting, are, as I have found lately, either in tempera altogether, or tempera with oil above. And I am disposed to think that ultimately tempera will be found the proper material for the greater number of most delightful subjects.

The subject, in the present instance, is a simple study of animal life in all its phases. I am quite sure that this is the meaning of the picture in Carpaccio's own mind. I suppose him to have been commissioned to paint the portraits of two Venetian ladies—that he did not altogether like his models, but yet felt himself bound to do his best for them, and contrived to do what perfectly satisfied them and himself too. He has painted their pretty faces and pretty shoulders, their pretty dresses and pretty jewels, their pretty ways and their pretty playmates—and what would they have more ?—he himself secretly laughing at them all the time, and intending the spectators of the future to laugh for ever.

It may be, however, that I err in supposing the picture a portrait commission. It may be simply a study for practice, gathering together every kind of thing which he could get to sit to him quietly, persuading the pretty ladies to sit to him in all their finery, and to keep their pets quiet as long as they could, while yet he gave value to this new group of studies in a certain unity of satire against the vices of society in his time.

Of this satirical purpose there cannot be question for a

moment, with any one who knows the general tone of the painter's mind, and the traditions among which he had been educated. In all the didactic painting of mediæval Christianity, the faultful luxury of the upper classes was symbolized by the knight with his falcon, and lady with her pet dog, both in splendid dress. This picture is only the elaboration of the well-recognized symbol of the lady with her pets; but there are two ladies—mother and daughter, I think—and six pets, a big dog, a little dog, a parroquet, a peahen, a little boy, and a china vase. The youngest of the women sits serene in her pride, her erect head pale against the dark sky—the elder is playing with the two dogs; the least, a white terrier, she is teaching to beg, holding him up by his fore-paws, with her left hand; in her right is a slender riding-whip, which the larger dog has the end of in his mouth, and will not let go—his mistress also having dropped a letter,* he puts his paw on that and will not let her pick it up, looking out of gentlest eyes in arch watchfulness to see how far it will please her that he should carry the jest. Behind him the green parroquet, red-eyed, lifts its little claw as if disliking the marble pavement; then behind the marble balustrade with gilded capitals, the bird and little boy are inlaid with glowing brown and red. Nothing of Hunt or Turner can surpass the plume painting of the bird; nor can Holbein surpass the precision, while he cannot equal the radiance, of the porcelain and jewellery.

To mark the satirical purpose of the whole, a pair of ladies' shoes are put in the corner, (the high-stilted shoe, being, in fact, a slipper on the top of a column,) which

* The painter's signature is on the supposed letter.

were the grossest and absurdest means of expressing
female pride in the fifteenth and following centuries.

In this picture, then, you may discern at once how Carpaccio learned his business as a painter, and to what consummate point he learned it.*

And now, if you have begun to feel the power of these
minor pictures, you can return to the Academy and take
up the St. Ursula series, on which, however, I find it
hopeless to reduce my notes to any available form at present:—the question of the influence of this legend on
Venetian life being involved with enquiries belonging
properly to what I am trying to do in "St. Mark's Rest."
This only you have to observe generally, that being meant
to occupy larger spaces, the St. Ursula pictures are very
unequal in interest, and many portions seem to me tired
work, while others are maintained by Mr. Murray to be
only by the hands of scholars. This, however, I can myself assert, that I never yet began to copy or examine any
portion of them without continually increasing admiration; while yet there are certain shortcomings and mor-
bid faults throughout, unaccountable, and rendering the
greater part of the work powerless for good to the general
public. Taken as a connected series, the varying personality of the saint destroys its interest totally. The girl
talking to her father in 539 is not the girl who dreams in
533; and the gentle little dreamer is still less like the se-
vere, stiffly dressed, and not in any supreme degree well

---

* Another Carpaccio, in the Correr Museum, of St. Mary and Elizabeth, is entirely lovely, though slighter in work; and the so called Mantegna, but more probably (according to Mr. Murray) early John Bellini,
—the Transfiguration,—full of majesty and earnestness. Note the inscribed "talk" with Moses and Elias,—" Have pity upon me, have pity
upon me, oh ye my friends."

favoured, bride, in 542; while the middle-aged woman,
without any claim to beauty **at all,** who occupies the principal place in the final Gloria, cannot by any effort of **imagination** be connected **with** the figure of the young girl
kneeling for the Pope's blessing in 546.

But indeed had the story **been as** consistently told as
the accessories **are** perfectly painted, there would have
been no occasion **for me now to be lecturing on** the beauties of Carpaccio. The public would long since have discovered them, and **adopted** him for **a** favourite. **That**
precisely **in the particulars** which would win popular attention, **the men whom it** would be most profitable for the
public to study **should so often** fail, becomes to me, as I
grow older, one of those deepest mysteries of life, which
I only can hope to have explained to me when my task of
interpretation **is** ended.

But, for the sake of Christian charity, **I** would ask
every generous Protestant **to pause** for a while before the
meeting under the Castle of **St.** Angelo, **(546).**

"Nobody **knows** anything about those old things," said
an English paterfamilias to **some** enquiring member of
his family, in the hearing of my assistant, then at work on
this picture. Which saying is indeed supremely true of us
nationally. But without requiring us to know anything,
this picture puts before us some certainties respecting mediæval Catholicism, which we shall do well to remember.

In the first place, you will find that all these bishops and
cardinals are evidently portraits. Their faces are too **varied**—too quiet—too complete—to have been invented by
even the mightiest invention. Carpaccio was simply taking the features of the priesthood of his time, throwing
aside, doubtless, here and there, matter of offence;—the

7

too settled gloom of one, the evident subtlety of another, the sensuality of a third ; but finding beneath all that, what was indeed the constitutional power and pith of their minds,—in the deep of them, rightly thoughtful, tender, and humble.

There is one curious little piece of satire on the fault of the Church in making cardinals of too young persons. The third, in the row of four behind St. Ursula, is a mere boy, very beautiful, but utterly careless of what is going on, and evidently no more fit to be a cardinal than a young calf would be. The stiffness of his white dress, standing up under his chin as if he had only put it on that day, draws especial attention to him.

The one opposite to him also, without this piece of white dress, seems to be a mere man of the world. But the others have all grave and refined faces. That of the Pope himself is quite exquisite in its purity, simple-heartedness, and joyful wonder at the sight of the child kneeling at his feet, in whom he recognizes one whom he is himself to learn of, and follow.

The more I looked at this picture, the more I became wonderstruck at the way the faith of the Christian Church has been delivered to us through a series of fables, which, partly meant as such, are over-ruled into expressions of truth—but how much truth, it is only by our own virtuous life that we can know. Only remember always in criticizing such a picture, that it no more means to tell you as a fact * that St. Ursula led this long procession from the sea and knelt thus before the Pope, than Mantegna's St. Sebastian means that the saint ever stood

* If it *had* been a fact, of course he would have liked it all the better, as in the picture of St. Stephen; but though only an idea, it must be realized to the full.

quietly and happily, stuck full of arrows. It is as much a
mythic symbol as the circles and crosses of the Carita;
but only Carpaccio carries out his symbol into delighted
realization, so that it begins to be absurd to us in the perceived impossibility. But it only signifies the essential
truth of joy in the Holy Ghost filling the whole body of
the Christian Church with visible inspiration, sometimes
in old men, sometimes in children; yet never breaking
the laws of established authority and subordination—the
greater saint blessed by the lesser, when the lesser is in
the higher place of authority, and all the common and
natural glories and delights of the world made holy by its
influence: field, and earth, and mountain, and sea, and
bright maiden's grace, and old men's quietness,—all in
one music of moving peace—the very procession of them
in their multitude like a chanted hymn—the purple stand-
ards drooping in the light air that yet can lift St. George's
gonfalon; * and the angel Michael alighting—himself seen
in vision instead of his statue—on the Angel's tower,
.sheathing his sword.

What I have to say respecting the picture that closes
the series, the martyrdom and funeral, is partly saddening,
partly depreciatory, and shall be reserved for another
place. The picture itself has been more injured and re-
painted than any other (the face of the recumbent figure
entirely so); and though it is full of marvellous passages,
I hope that the general traveller will seal his memory of
Carpaccio in the picture last described.

* It is especially to be noted with Carpaccio, and perhaps more in
this than any other of the series, that he represents the beauty of religion always in animating the present world, and never gives the charm
to the clear far-away sky which is so constant in Florentine sacred pictures.

THE PLACE OF DRAGONS.

JAMES REDDIE ANDERSON, M.A.

PREFACE.

Among the many discomforts of advancing age, which no one understands till he feels them, there is one which I seldom have heard complained of, and which, therefore, I find unexpectedly disagreeable. I knew, by report, that when I grew old I should most probably wish to be young again; and, very certainly, be ashamed of much that I had done, or omitted, in the active years of life. I was prepared for sorrow in the loss of friends by death; and for pain, in the loss of myself, by weakness or sickness. These, and many other minor calamities, I have been long accustomed to anticipate; and therefore to read, in preparation for them, the confessions of the weak, and the consolations of the wise.

But, as the time of rest, or of departure, approaches me, not only do many of the evils I had heard of, and prepared for, present themselves in more grievous shapes than I had expected; but one which I had scarcely ever heard of, torments me increasingly every hour.

I had understood it to be in the order of things that the aged should lament their vanishing life as an instrument they had never used, now to be taken away from them; but not as an instrument, only then perfectly tempered and sharpened, and snatched out of their hands at the instant they could have done some real service with it. Whereas, my own feeling, now, is that everything which has hitherto happened to me, or been done by me, whether well or ill, has been fitting me to take greater fortune more prudently, and do better work more thoroughly. And just when I seem to be coming out of school—very sorry to have been such a foolish boy, yet having taken a prize or two, and expecting to enter now upon some more serious business than cricket,—I am dismissed by the Master I hoped to serve, with a—"That's all I want of you, sir."

I imagine the sorrowfulness of these feelings must be abated, in the minds of most men, by a pleasant vanity in their hope of being remembered as the discoverers, at least, of some important truth, or the founders of some exclusive system called after their own names. But I have never applied myself to discover anything, being content to praise what had already been discovered; and the only doctrine or system peculiar to me is the abhorrence of all that is doctrinal instead of demonstrable, and of all that is systematic instead of useful: so that *no true* disciple of mine will ever be a "Ruskinian"!—he will follow, not me, but the instincts of his own soul, and the guidance of its Creator. Which, though not a sorrowful subject of contemplation in itself, leaves me none of the common props and crutches of halting pride. I know myself to be a true master, because my pupils are well on the way to do better than I have done; but there is not always a sense of extreme pleasure in watching their advance, where one has no more strength, though more than ever the will, to companion them.

Not *always*—be it again confessed; but when I first read the legend of St. George, which here follows, my eyes grew wet with tears of true delight; first, in the knowledge of so many beautiful things, at once given to me; and then in the surety of the wide good that the work thus begun would spring up into, in ways before wholly unconceived by me. It was like coming to the brow of some healthy moorland, where here and there one had watched, or helped, the reaper of some patch of thinly scattered corn; and seeing suddenly a great plain white to the harvest, far as the horizon. That the first-fruits of it might be given in no manner of self-exaltation —Fors has determined that my young scholar should have his part of mortification as well as I, just in the degree in which either of us may be mortified in the success of others. For we both thought that the tracing of this chain of tradition in the story of St. George was ours alone; and that we had rather to apprehend the doubt of our result, than the dispute of our originality. Nor was it, indeed, without extreme discomfiture and vexation that after I had been hindered from publishing this paper for upwards of ten months from the time it was first put into my hands, I read, on a bright autumn morning at Brant-wood, when I expected the author's visit, (the first he had made to me in my own house,) a paragraph in the "Spec-tator," giving abstract of exactly the same historical state-ments, made by a French antiquary, M. Clermont-Ganneau.

I am well assured that Professor Airey was not more grieved, though I hope he was more conscience-stricken, for his delay in the publication of Mr. Adams' calcula-tions, than I was, for some days after seeing this antici-pation of my friend's discoveries. He relieved my mind himself, after looking into the matter, by pointing out to me that the original paper had been read by M. Clermont-Ganneau, before the Académie des Inscriptions et Belles-lettres of Paris, two months before his own investigations

7*

had begun, and that all question of priority was, therefore, at an end. It remained for us only to surrender, both of us, what complacency we should have had in first announcing these facts; and to take a nobler pleasure in the confirmation afforded of their truth by the coincidence, to a degree of accuracy which neither of us had ever known take place before in the work of two entirely independent investigators, between M. Clermont-Ganneau's conclusions and our own. I therefore desired my friend to make no alterations in his paper as it then stood, and to make no reference himself to the French author, but to complete his own course of investigation independently, as it was begun. We shall have some bits all to ourselves, before we have done; and in the meantime give reverent thanks to St. George, for his help, to France as well as to England, in enabling the two nations to read together the truth of his tradition, on the distant clouds of Heaven and Time.

Mr. Anderson's work remains entirely distinct, in its interpretation of Carpaccio's picture by this tradition, and since at the mouth of two—or *three*, witnesses shall a word be established, Carpaccio himself thus becomes the third, and the chief, witness to its truth; and to the power of it on the farthest race of the Knights of Venice.

The present essay treats only of the first picture in the chapel of St. George. I hope it may now be soon followed by its author's consecutive studies of the other subjects, in which he has certainly no priority of effort to recognize, and has, with the help of the good Saints and no other persons, done all that we shall need.

J. Ruskin.

Brantwood,
  26th January, 1878.

THE PLACE OF DRAGONS.

"'Εννοήσας ὅτι τὸν ποιητὴν δέοι, εἴπερ μέλλοι ποιητὴς εἶναι, ποιεῖν μύθους ἀλλ' οὐ λόγους."—*Plat. Phædo*, 61, B.

ON the eve of the Feast of the Annunciation, in the year of Christ 1452, the Council of Ten, by decree, permitted certain Dalmatians settled in Venice to establish a Lay Brotherhood, called of St. George and of St. Tryphonius. The brothers caused to be written in illuminated letters on the first pages of their minute book their "memorandum of association." They desired to "hold united in sacred bonds men of Dalmatian blood, to render homage to God and to His saints by charitable endeavours and religious ceremonies, and to help by holy sacrifices the souls of brothers alive and dead." The brotherhood gave, and continues to give, material support to the poor of Dalmatian blood in Venice; money to the old, and education to the young. For prayer and adoration it built the chapel known as St. George's of the Sclavonians. In this chapel, during the first decade of the sixteenth century, Carpaccio painted a series of pictures. First, three from the story of St. Jerome—not that St. Jerome was officially a patron of the brothers, but a fellow-countryman, and therefore, as it were, an ally;—then three from the story of St. George, one from that of St. Tryphonius, and two smaller from the Gospel History. Allowing for doorways, window, and altar, these nine pictures fill the circuit of the chapel walls.

Those representing St. George are placed opposite those of St. Jerome. In the ante-chapel of the Ducal Palace, Tintoret, who studied, not without result otherwise, these pictures of Carpaccio's, has placed the same saints over against each other. To him, as to Carpaccio, they represented the two sides, practical and contemplative, of faithful life. This balance we still, though with less completeness, signify by the linked names of Martha and Mary, and Plato has expressed it fully by the respective functions assigned in his ideal state to philosophers and guardians. The seer "able to grasp the eternal," "spectator of all time and of all existence,"—you may see him on your right as you enter this chapel,—recognizes and declares God's Law: the guardian obeys, enforces, and, if need be, fights for it.

St. George, Husbandman by name, and "Τροπαιοφόρος," Triumphant Warrior, by title, secures righteous peace, turning his spear into a pruning-hook for the earthly nature of man. He is also to be known as "Μεγαλομάρτυρ," by his deeds, the great witness for God in the world, and "τῶν ἀθλητῶν ὁ μέγας Ταξιάρχης," marshal and leader of those who strive to obtain an incorruptible crown.* St. Jerome, the seer, learned also in all the wisdom of the heathen, is, as Plato tells us such a man should be. Lost in his longing after "the universal law that knits human things with divine," † he shows

* These titles are taken from the earliest (Greek) records of him. The last corresponds to that of Baron Bradwardine's revered "Mareschal-Duke."

† Plat. Rep., VI. 486 A.

himself gentle and without fear, having no terror even of
death.* In the second picture on our right here we may
see with how great quiet the old man has laid himself
down to die, even such a pillow beneath his head as was
under Jacob's upon that night of vision by the place
which he thenceforward knew to be the "House of God,"
though "the name of it was called 'Separation' † at the
first." ‡ The fantastic bilingual interpretation of Jerome's name given in the "Golden Legend," standard of
mediæval mythology, speaks to the same effect: "Hie-
ronimus, quod est Sanctum Nemus," Holy Grove, "a ne-
more ubi aliquando conversatus est," from that one in
which he sometime had his walk—"Se dedit et sacri ne-
moris perpalluit umbra," ‖ but not beneath the laurels of
"l'un giogo de Parnaso," § to whose inferior summit, only,
Dante in that line alludes, nor now under olive boughs—

" where the Attick bird
Trills her thick-warbled notes the summer long,"

but where, once on a winter night, shepherds in their

* Plat. Rep., **VI. 486 B.**

† Luz. This **word stands also for** the almond tree, flourishing when
desire fails, and "man goeth to his long home."

‡ In the **21st** and 22nd Cantos of the "Paradise," Dante, too, con-
nects the dream of Jacob with the ascetic, living where "e consecrato
un ermo, Che suole esser disposto a sola latria." This is in a sphere of
heaven where "la dolce sinfonia del Paradiso" is heard by mortal ears
only as overmastering thunder, and where the pilgrim is taught that no
created vision, not the seraph's "che in Dio piu l'occhio ha fisso" may
read that eternal statute by whose appointment spirits of the saints go
forth upon their Master's **business** and return to Him again.

‖ Dante, "Eclogues," i. **30.**

§ Dante, "Par." **I. 16.**

vigil heard other singing, where the palm bearer of burdens, witness of victorious hope, offers to every man, for
the gathering, fruit unto everlasting life. " Ad Bethleem oppidum remeavit, ubi, prudens animal, ad præsepe
Domini se obtulit permansurum." " He went, as though
home, to the town of Bethlehem, and like a wise domestic creature presented himself at his Master's manger to
abide there."

After the pictures of St. George comes that of St. Tryphonius, telling how the prayer of a little child shall con-
quer the basilisk of earthly pride, though the soldier's
spear cannot overthrow *this* monster, nor maiden's zone
bind him. After the picture of St. Jerome we are given
the Calling of Matthew, in which Carpaccio endeavours
to declare how great joy fills the fugitive servant of Riches
when at last he does homage as true man of another
Master. Between these two is set the central picture of
the nine, small, dark itself, and in a dark corner, in ar-
rangement following pretty closely the simple tradition of
earlier Venetian masters. The scene is an untilled garden—the subject, the Agony of our Lord.

The prominent feature of the stories Carpaccio has
chosen—setting aside at present the two gospel incidents
—is that, though heartily Christian, they are historically
drawn quite as much from Greek as from mediæval
mythology. Even in the scenes from St. Jerome's life, a
well-known classical tale, which mingled with his legend,
is introduced, and all the paintings contain much ancient
religious symbolism. St. Tryphonius' conquest of the
basilisk is, as we shall see, almost purely a legend of
Apollo. From the middle ages onwards it has been often
remarked how closely the story of St. George and the

Dragon resembles that of Perseus and Andromeda. It does not merely resemble,—it *is* that story.

The earliest and central shrine of St. George,—his church, famous during the crusades, at Lydda,—rose by the stream which Pausanias, in the second century, saw running still "red as blood," because Perseus had bathed there after his conquest of the sea monster. From the neighbouring town of Joppa, as Pliny tells us, the skeleton of that monster was brought by M. Scaurus to Rome in the first century B.C. St. Jerome was shown on this very coast a rock known by tradition as that to which Andromeda had been bound. Before his day Josephus had seen in that rock the holes worn by her fetters.

In the place chosen by fate for this the most famous and finished example of harmony between the old faith and the new there is a strange double piece of real mythology. Many are offended when told that with the best teaching of the Christian Church Gentile symbolism and story have often mingled. Some still lament vanished dreams of the world's morning, echo the

"Voice of weeping heard, and loud lament,"

by woodland altar and sacred thicket. But Lydda was the city where St. Peter raised from death to doubly-marvellous service that loved garment-maker, full of good works, whose name was Wild Roe—Greek * type of dawn with its pure visions. And Lydda "was nigh unto Joppa," † where was let down from heaven the mystic

---

* The Hebrew poets, too, knew "the Hind of the glow of dawn."

† Near Joppa the Moslem (who also reverences St. George) sees the field of some great final contest between the Evil and the Good, upon

sheet, full of every kind of living creature, (this, centuries before, a symbol familiar to the farthest east, *) for lasting witness to the faithful that through his travailing creation God has appointed all things to be helpful and holy to man, has made nothing common or unclean.

There is a large body of further evidence proving the origin of the story of St. George and the Dragon from that of Perseus. The names of certain of the persons concerned in both coincide. Secondary, or later variations in the place of the fight appear alike in both legends. For example, the scene of both is sometimes laid in Phœnicia, north of Joppa. But concerning this we may note that a mythologist of the age of Augustus,† recounting this legend, is careful to explain that the name of Joppa had since been changed to Phœnice. The instance of most value, however—because connected with a singular identity of local names—is that account which takes both Perseus and St. George to the Nile delta. The Greek name of Lydda was Diospolis. Now St. Jerome speaks strangely of Alexandria as also called Diospolis, and there certainly was a Diospolis (later Lydda) near Alexandria, where "alone in Egypt," Strabo tells us, "men did not venerate the crocodile, but held it in dishonour as most hateful of living things." One of the "Crocodile towns" of Egypt was close by this. Curiously enough, considering the locality, there was also a "Crocodile-town" a short distance north of Joppa. In Thebes,

whom the ends of the world shall have come—a contest surely that will require the presence of our warrior-marshal.

* Compare the illustrations on p. 44 of Didron's "Iconographie Chrétienne" (English translation, p. 41).

† Conon. Narr., XL. .

too, the greater Diospolis, there was a shrine of Perseus, and near it another Κροκοδείλων Πόλις. This persistent recurrence of the name Diospolis probably points to Perseus' original identity with the sun—noblest birth of the Father of Lights. In its Greek form that name was, of course, of comparatively late imposition, but we may well conceive it to have had reference * to a local terminology and worship much more ancient. It is not unreasonable to connect too the Diospolis of Cappadocia, a region so frequently and mysteriously referred to as that of St. George's birth.

Further, the stories both of Perseus and of St. George are curiously connected with the Persians; but this matter, together with the saint's Cappadocian nationality, will fall to be considered in relation to a figure in the last of Carpaccio's three pictures, which will open up to us the earliest history and deepest meaning of the myth.

The stories of the fight given by Greeks and Christians are almost identical. There is scarcely an incident in it told by one set of writers but occurs in the account given by some member or members of the other set, even to the crowd of distant spectators Carpaccio has so dwelt upon, and to the votive altars raised above the body of the monster, with the stream of healing that flowed beside them. And while both accounts say how the saved nations rendered thanks to the Father in heaven, we are told that the heathen placed, beside His altar, altars to the Maiden Wisdom and to Hermes, while the Christians placed altars dedicated to the Maiden Mother and to George. Even Medusa's head did not come amiss to the mediæval artist, but set in the saint's hand became his own, fit indication

* Compare the name Heliopolis given both to Baalbeck and On·

of the death by which he should afterwards glorify God.
And here we may probably trace the original error—if,
indeed, to be called an error—by which the myth concerning Perseus was introduced into the story of our soldier-
saint of the East.   From the fifth century to the fifteenth,
mythologists nearly all give, and usually with approval,
an interpretation of the word " gorgon " which makes
it identical in meaning and derivation with " George."
When comparatively learned persons, taught too in this
special subject, accepted such an opinion and insisted upon
it, we cannot be surprised if their contemporaries, unedu-
cated, or educated only in the Christian mysteries, took
readily a similar view, especially when we consider the
wild confusion in mediæval minds concerning the spelling
of classical names.   Now just as into the legend of St.
Hippolytus there was introduced a long episode manifest-
ly derived from some disarranged and misunderstood series of paintings or sculptures concerning the fate of the
Greek Hippolytus,—and this is by no means a singular
example, the name inscribed on the work of art being
taken as evidence that it referred to the only bearer of
that name then thought of—so, in all probability, it came
about with St. George.   People at Lydda far on into
Christian times would know vaguely, and continue to tell
the story, how long ago under that familiar cliff the dragon was slain and the royal maid released.   Then some
ruined fresco or vase painting of the event would exist,
half forgotten, with the names of the characters written
after Greek fashion near them in the usual superbly errant
caligraphy.   The Gorgon's name could scarcely fail to be
prominent in a series of pictures from Perseus' history,
or in this scene as an explanation of the head in his hand.

A Christian pilgrim, or hermit, his heart full of the great saint, whose name as "Triumphant" filled the East, would, when he had spelt out the lettering, at once exclaim, "Ah, here is recorded another of my patron's victories." The probability of this is enhanced by the appearance in St. George's story of names whose introduction seems to require a similar explanation. But we shall find that the battle with the dragon, though not reckoned among St. George's deeds before the eleventh or twelfth century, is entirely appropriate to the earliest sources of his legend.

One other important parallel between Perseus and St. George deserves notice, though it does not bear directly upon these pictures. Both are distinguished by their burnished shields. The hero's was given him by Athena, that, watching in it there fleeted figure of the Gorgon,* he might strike rightly with his sickle-sword, nor need to meet in face the mortal horror of her look. The saint's bright shield rallied once and again a breaking host of crusaders, as they seemed to see it blaze in their van under Antioch † wall, and by the breaches of desecrated Zion. But his was a magic mirror; work of craftsmen more cunning than might obey the Queen of Air. Turned to visions of terror and death, it threw back by law of diviner optics an altered image—the crimson blazon of its cross.‡ So much for the growth of the dragon legend,

---

* The allegorising Platonists interpret Medusa as a symbol of man's sensual nature. This we shall find to be Carpaccio's view of the dragon of St. George.

† Acts xi. 26.

‡ Compare the strange reappearance of the Æginetan Athena as St. John on the Florin. There the arm that bore the shield now with pointed finger gives emphasis and direction to the word " Behold."

fragment of a most ancient faith, widely spread and variously localised, thus made human by Greek, and passionately spiritual by Christian, art.

We shall see later that Perseus is not St. George's only blood-relation among the powers of earlier belief; but for Englishmen there may be a linked association, if more difficult to trace through historic descent, yet, in its perfect harmony, even more pleasantly strange. The great heroic poem which remains to us in the tongue of our Anglo-Saxon ancestors—intuitive creation and honourable treasure for ever of simple English minds—tells of a warrior whose names, like St. George's, are "Husbandman" and "Glorious," whose crowning deed was done in battle with the poisonous drake. Even a figure very important in St. George's history—one we shall meet in the third of these pictures—is in this legend not without its representative—that young kinsman of the Saxon hero, "among the faithless" earls "faithful only he," who holds before the failing eyes of his lord the long rusted helm and golden standard, "wondrous in the grasp," and mystic vessels of ancient time, treasure redeemed at last by a brave man's blood from the vaulted cavern of the "Twilight Flyer." For Beowulf indeed slays the monster, but wins no princess, and dies of the fiery venom that has scorched his limbs in the contest. Him there awaited such fires alone—seen from their bleak promontory afar over northern seas—as burned once upon the ridge of Œta, his the Heraklean crown of poplar leaves only, blackened without by the smoke of hell, and on the inner side washed white with the sweat of a labourer's brow.* It is a wilder form

* There was in his People's long lament for Beowulf one word about the hidden future, "when he must go forth from the body to become

of the great story told by seers* who knew only the terror
of nature and the daily toil of men, and the doom that is
over these for each of us. The royal maiden for ever set
free, the sprinkling of pure water unto eternal life,—this
only such eyes may discern as by happier fate have also
rested upon tables whose divine blazon is the law of
heaven ; such hearts alone conceive, as, trained in some
holy city of God, have among the spirits of just men
made perfect, learned to love His commandment.

Such, then, was the venerable belief which Carpaccio
set himself to picture in the Chapel of St. George. How
far he knew its wide reign and ancient descent, or how
far, without recognising these, he intuitively acted as the
knowledge would have led him, and was conscious of
lighting up his work by Gentile learning and symbolism,
must to us be doubtful. It is not doubtful that, whether
with open eyes, or in simple obedience to the traditions
of his training, or, as is most likely, loyal as well in wisdom as in humility, he did so illumine it, and very glo-
riously. But painting this glory, he paints with it the

. . . . " What to become we shall not know, for fate has struck out
just the four letters that would have told us.

* " Beowulf " was probably composed by a poet nearly contemporary
with Bede. The dragon victory was not yet added to the glories of St.
George. Indeed, Pope Gelasius, in Council, more than a couple of centuries before, had declared him to be one of those saints " whose names
are justly revered among men, but whose deeds are known to God
only." Accordingly the Saxon teacher invokes him somewhat vaguely
thus :—

> " Invicto mundum qui sanguine temnis[1]
> Infinita refers, Georgi Sancte, trophæa ! "

Yet even in these words we see a reverence similar to Carpaccio's for
St. George as patron of purity. And the deeds " known to God alone "
were in His good time revealed to those to whom it pleased Him.

peace that over the king-threatened cradle of another
Prince than Perseus, was proclaimed to the heavy-laden.

The first picture on the left hand as we enter the chapel
shows St. George on horseback, in battle with the Dragon.
Other artists, even Tintoret,* are of opinion that the Saint
rode a white horse. The champion of Purity must, they
hold, have been carried to victory by a charger ethereal
and splendid as a summer cloud. Carpaccio believed that
his horse was a dark brown. He knew that this colour is
generally the mark of greatest strength and endurance;
he had no wish to paint here an ascetic's victory over the
flesh. St. George's warring is in the world, and for it;
he is the enemy of its desolation, the guardian of its
peace; and all vital force of the lower Nature he shall
have to bear him into battle; submissive indeed to the
spur, bitted and bridled for obedience, yet honourably
decked with trappings whose studs and bosses are fair car-
ven faces. But though of colour prosaically useful; this
horse has a deeper kinship with the air. Many of the
ancient histories and vase-paintings tell us that Perseus,
when he saved Andromeda, was mounted on Pegasus.
Look now here at the mane and tail, swept still back upon
the wind, though already the passionate onset has been
brought to sudden pause in that crash of encounter.
Though the flash of an earthly fire be in his eye, its force
in his limbs—though the clothing of his neck be Chtho-
nian thunder—this steed is brother, too, to that one, born
by farthest ocean wells, whose wild mane and sweeping
wings stretch through the firmament as light is breaking
over earth. More; these masses of billowy hair tossed
upon the breeze of heaven are set here for a sign that

---

* In the ante-chapel of the Ducal Palace.

this, though but one of the beasts that perish, has the
roots of his strong nature in the power of heavenly life,
and is now about His business who is Lord of heaven and
Father of men. The horse is thus, as we shall see, opposed to certain other signs, meant for our learning, in
the dream of horror round this monster's den.*

St. George, armed to his throat, sits firmly in the sad-
dle. All the skill gained in a chivalric youth, all the
might of a soldier's manhood, he summons for this strange
tourney, stooping slightly and gathering his strength as
he drives the spear-point straight between his enemy's
jaws. His face is very fair, at once delicate and power-
ful, well-bred in the fullest bearing of the words; a Plan-
tagenet face in general type, but much refined. The
lower lip is pressed upwards, the brow knit, in anger and
disgust partly, but more in care—and care not so much
concerning the fight's ending, as that this thrust in it shall
now be rightly dealt. His hair flows in bright golden
ripples, strong as those of a great spring whose up-welling
waters circle through some clear pool, but it breaks at last
to float over brow and shoulders in tendrils of living
light.† Had Carpaccio been aware that St. George and
Perseus are, in this deed, one; had he even held, as surely
as Professor Müller finds reason to do, that at first Perseus was but the sun in his strength—for very name, being called the " Brightly-Burning "—this glorious head
could not have been, more completely than it is, made the

* This cloudlike effect is through surface rubbing perhaps more
marked now than Carpaccio intended, but must always have been most
noticeable. It produces a very striking resemblance to the Pegasus or
the Ram of Phrixus on Greek vases.

† At his martyrdom St. George was hung up by his hair to be
scourged.

centre of light in the picture. In Greek works of art, **as**
a rule, **Perseus, when** he rescues Andromeda, continues to
wear the peaked **Phrygian cap, dark** helmet of Hades,[*]
by whose virtue he moved, · invisible, upon Medusa
through coiling mists of dawn. Only after victory might
he unveil his brightness. But about George from the
first is no shadow. Creeping thing of keenest eye **shall**
not see that splendour which is so manifest, **nor with**
guile spring upon it unaware, to its darkening. **Such**
knowledge alone for the dragon—dim sense as of **a horse**
with its rider, moving to the fatal lair, hope, pulseless,—
not of heart, but of talon and maw—that here is yet
another victim, then only **between** his teeth that keen
lance-point, thrust far before the **Holy** Apparition at
whose rising the Power of the Vision of Death waxes
faint and drops those terrible wings that bore under their
shadow, not healing, but wounds **for men.**

The spear pierces the base of the dragon's brain, its
point penetrating right through and standing out at the
back of the head just above its junction with the spine.
The shaft breaks in the shock between the dragon's jaws.
This shivering of St. George's spear is almost always em-
phasized in pictures of him—sometimes, as here, in act,
oftener by position of the splintered fragments prominent
in the foreground. This is no tradition of ancient art,
but a purely mediæval incident, yet not, I believe, merely
the vacant reproduction of a sight become familiar to the
spectator of tournaments. The spear was type of the
strength of human wisdom. This checks the enemy in
his attack, subdues him partly, yet is shattered, having
done so much, and of no help in perfecting the victory **or**

* Given by Hermes (Chthonios).

in reaping its reward of joy. But at the Saint's "loins, girt about with truth," there hangs his holier weapon—the Sword of the Spirit, which is the Word of God.

The Dragon * is bearded like a goat,† and essentially a thorny ‡ creature. Every ridge of his body, wings, and head, bristles with long spines, keen, sword-like, of an earthy brown colour or poisonous green. But the most truculent-looking of all is a short, strong, hooked one at the back of his head, close to where the spear-point protrudes.§ These thorns are partly the same vision—though seen with even clearer eyes, dreamed by a heart yet more tender—as Spenser saw in the troop of urchins coming up with the host of other lusts against the Castle of Temperance. They are also symbolic as weeds whose deadly growth brings the power of earth to waste and chokes its good. These our Lord of spiritual husbandmen must for preliminary task destroy. The agricultural process consequent on this first step in tillage we shall see in the next picture, whose subject is the triumph of the ploughshare sword, as the subject of this one is the triumph of the pruning hook spear.‖ To an Italian of Carpaccio's time, further, spines—etymologically connected in Greek and

---

* It should be noticed that St. George's dragon is never human-headed, as often St. Michael's.

† So the Theban dragon on a vase, to be afterwards referred to.

‡ The following are Lucian's words concerning the monster slain by Perseus, " Καὶ τὸ μὲν ἐπειδὶ πεφρικὸς ταῖς ἀκάνθαις καὶ δεδιττόμενον τῷ χάσματι."

§ I do not know the meaning of this here. It bears a striking resemblance to the crests of the dragon of Triptolemus on vases. These crests signify primarily the springing blade of corn. That, here, has become like iron.

‖ For " pruning-hooks " in our version, the Vulgate reads "ligones" —tools for preparatory clearance.

8

Latin, as in English, with the backbone—were an acknowledged symbol of the lust of the flesh, whose defeat the artist has here set himself to paint. The mighty coiling tail, as of a giant eel,* carries out the portraiture. For this, loathsome as the body is full of horror, takes the place of the snails ranked by Spenser in line beside his urchins. Though the monster, half-rampant, rises into air, turning claw and spike and tooth towards St. George, we are taught by this grey abomination twisting in the slime of death that the threatened destruction is to be dreaded not more for its horror than for its shame.

Behind the dragon lie, naked, with dead faces turned heavenwards, two corpses—a youth's and a girl's, eaten away from the feet to the middle, the flesh hanging at the waist in loathsome rags torn by the monster's teeth. The man's thigh and upper-arm bones snapped across and sucked empty of marrow, are turned to us for special sign of this destroyer's power. The face, foreshortened, is drawn by death and decay into the ghastly likeness of an ape's.† The girl's face—seen in profile—is quiet and still beautiful; her long hair is heaped as for a pillow under

---

* The eel was Venus' selected beast-shape in the "Flight of the Gods." Boccaccio has enlarged upon the significance of this. Gen. Deor. IV. 68. One learns from other sources that a tail was often symbol of sensuality.

† In the great Botticelli of the National Gallery, known as Mars and Venus, but almost identical with the picture drawn afterwards by Spenser of the Bower of Acrasia, the sleeping youth wears an expression, though less strongly marked, very similar to that of this dead face here. Such brutish paralysis is with scientific accuracy made special to the male. It may be noticed that the power of venomously wounding, expressed by Carpaccio through the dragon's spines, is in the Botticelli signified by the swarm of hornets issuing from the tree-trunk by the young man's head.

her head. It does not grow like St. George's, in living ripples, but lies in fantastic folds, that have about them a savour, not of death only, but of corruption. For all its pale gold they at once carry back one's mind to Turner's Pytho, where the arrow of Apollo strikes him in the midst, and, piercing, reveals his foulness. Round her throat cling a few torn rags, these only remaining of the white garment that clothed her once. Carpaccio was a diligent student of ancient mythology. Boccaccio's very learned book on the Gods was the standard classical dictionary of those days in Italy. It tells us how the Cyprian Venus—a mortal princess in reality, Boccaccio holds —to cover her own disgrace led the maidens of her country to the sea-sands, and, stripping them there, tempted them to follow her in shame. I suspect Carpaccio had this story in his mind, and meant here to reveal in true dragon aspect the Venus that once seemed fair, to show by this shore the fate of them that follow her. It is to be noticed that the dead man is an addition made by Carpaccio to the old story. Maidens of the people, the legend-writers knew, had been sacrificed before the Princess; but only he, filling the tale—like a cup of his country's fairly fashioned glass—full of the wine of profitable teaching, is aware that men have often come to these yellow sands to join there in the dance of death—not only, nor once for all, this Saint who clasped hands with Victory. Two ships in the distance—one stranded, with rigging rent or fallen, the other moving prosperously with full sails on its course—symbolically repeat this thought.*

Frogs clamber about the corpse of the man, lizards about the woman. Indeed for shells and creeping things

* "The many fail, the one succeeds."

this place where strangers lie slain and unburied would have been to the good Palissy a veritable and valued potter's field. But to every one of these cold and scaly creatures a special symbolism was attached by the science—not unwisely dreaming—of Carpaccio's day. They are, each one, painted here to amplify and press home the picture's teaching. These lizards are born of a dead man's flesh, these snakes of his marrow : * and adders, the most venomous, are still only lizards ripened witheringly from loathsome flower into poisonous fruit. The frogs †—symbols, Pierius tells us, of imperfection and shamelessness—are in transfigured form those Lycian husbandmen whose foul words mocked Latona, whose feet defiled the wells of water she thirsted for, as the veiled mother painfully journeyed with those two babes on her arm, of whom one should be Queen of Maidenhood, the other, Lord of Light, and Guardian of the Ways of Men.‡ This subtle association between batrachians and love declining to sense lay very deep in the Italian mind. In "Ariadne Florentina" there are two engravings from Botticelli of Venus, as a star floating through heaven and as foam-born rising from the sea. Both pictures are most subtly beautiful, yet in the former the lizard likeness shows itself distinctly in the face, and a lizard's tail appears in manifest form as pendulous crest of the chariot, while in the latter not only contours of profile and back, § but the selected attitude of

* " The silver cord " not " loosed " in God's peace, but thus devilishly quickened.

† Compare the " unclean spirits come out of the mouth of the dragon," in Revelation.

‡ Ἀγυιεύς.

§ Compare the account of the Frog's hump, " Ariadne Florentina," p. 93.

the goddess, bent and half emergent, with hand resting not over firmly upon the level shore, irresistibly recall a frog.

In the foreground, between St. George and the Dragon, a spotted lizard labours at the task set Sisyphus in hell for ever. Sisyphus, the cold-hearted **and** shifty son of Æolus,* stained in life by nameless lust, received his mocking doom of toil, partly for his treachery—winning this only in the end,—partly because **he opposed the** divine conception of the Æacid race; but above all, **as penalty** for the attempt to elude the fate of death "that is appointed alike for all," by refusal for his own body of **that** " sowing in corruption," against which a deeper furrow is prepared by the last of husbandmen with whose labour each of us has on earth to do. Then, finding that Carpaccio has had in his mind one scene of Tartarus, we may believe the corpse in the background, torn by carrion-birds, to be not merely a meaningless incident of horror, but a reminiscence of enduring punishment avenging upon Tityus † the insulted purity of Artemis. ‡

The coiled adder is the familiar symbol of eternity, here meant either **to** seal for the defeated their fate as final, or to hint, with something of Turner's sadness, that this is a battle not gained "once for ever " and " for all," but to be fought anew by every son of man, while, for each, defeat shall be deadly, and victory still most hard, though an armed Angel of the Victory of God be our

* Compare Pindar's use of αἰόλος as a fit adjective for ψεῦδος, Nem viii. 43.

† " Terræ omniparentis alumnum."

‡ Or, as the story is otherwise given, of the mother of Artemis, as in the case of the Lycian peasants above.

marshal and leader in the contest. A further comparison with Turner is suggested by the horse's skull between us and Saint George. A similar skeleton is prominent in the corresponding part of the foreground in the "Jason" of the Liber Studiorum. But Jason clambers to victory on foot, allows no charger to bear him in the fight. Turner, more an antique * Hellene than a Christian prophet, had, as all the greatest among the Greeks, neither vision nor hope of any more perfect union between lower and higher nature by which that inferior creation, groaning now with us in pain, should cease to be type of the mortal element, which seems to shame our soul as basing it in clay, and, with that element, become a temple-platform, lifting man's life towards heaven.†

With Turner's adder, too, springing immortal from the Python's wound, we cannot but connect this other adder of Carpaccio's, issuing from the white skull of a great snake. Adders, according to an old fancy, were born from the jaws of their living mother. Supernatural horror attaches to this symbolic one, writhing out from between the teeth of that ophidian death's-head. And the plague, not yet fully come forth, but already about *its* father's business, venomously fastens on a frog, type of

---

* Hamlet, V. ii. 352.

† Pegasus and the immortal horses of Achilles, born like Pegasus by the ocean wells, are always to be recognized as spiritual creatures, not —as St. George's horse here—earthly creatures, though serving and manifesting divine power. Compare too the fate of Argus (Homer, Od., XVII.) In the great Greek philosophies, similarly, we find a realm of formless shadow eternally unconquered by sacred order, offering a contrast to the modern systems which aim at a unity to be reached, if not by reason, at least by what one may not inaccurately call an act of faith.

the sinner whose degradation is but the beginning of punishment. So soon the worm that dies not is also upon him—in its fang Circean poison to make the victim one with his plague, as in that terrible circle those, afflicted, whom "vita bestial piacque e non humana."

Two spiral shells * lie on the sand, in shape related to each other as frog to lizard, or as Spenser's urchins, spoken of above, to his snails. One is round and short, with smooth viscous-looking lip, turned over, and lying towards the spectator. The other is finer in form, and of a kind noticeable for its rows of delicate spines. But, since the dweller in this one died, the waves of many a long-fallen tide rolling on the shingle have worn it almost smooth, as you may see its fellows to-day by hundreds along Lido shore. Now such shells were, through heathen ages innumerable and over many lands, holy things, because of their whorls moving from left to right † in some mysterious sympathy, it seemed, with the sun in his daily course through heaven. Then as the open clam-shell was special symbol of Venus, so these became of the Syrian Venus, Ashtaroth, Ephesian Artemis, queen, not of purity but of abundance, Mylitta, ἥτις ποτ' ἐστὶν, the many named and widely worshipped.‡ In Syrian figures still existing she bears just such a shell in her hand. Later writers, with whom the source of this symbolism was forgotten, accounted for it, partly by imaginative instinct, partly by

* Ovid associates shells with the enemy of Andromeda, but regarding it as a very ancient and fishlike monster, plants them on its back—

"terga cavis super obsita conchis."—*Ov. Met.*, IV. 724.

† In India, for the same reason, one of the leading marks of the Buddha's perfection was his hair, thus spiral.

‡ Compare the curious tale about the Echeneis. Pliny, Hist. Nat., IX. 25. "De echeneide ejusque naturâ mirabili."

fanciful invention concerning the nature and way of life of these creatures. But there is here yet a further reference, since from such shells along the Syrian coast was crushed out, sea-purple and scarlet, the juice of the Tyrian dye. And the power of sensual delight throned in the chief places of each merchant city, decked her "stately bed" with coverings whose tincture was the stain of that baptism.* The shells are empty now, devoured—lizards on land or sea-shore are ever to such "inimicissimum genus" †—or wasted in the deep. For the ripples ‡ that have thrown and left them on the sand are a type of the lusts of men, that leap up from the abyss, surge over the shore of life, and fall in swift ebb, leaving desolation behind.

Near the coiled adder is planted a withered human head. The sinews and skin of the neck spread, and clasp the ground—as a zoophyte does its rock—in hideous mimicry of an old tree's knotted roots. Two feet and legs, torn off by the knee, lean on this head, one against the brow and the other behind. The scalp is bare and withered. These things catch one's eye on the first glance at the picture, and though so painful are made thus prominent as giving the key to a large part of its symbolism. Later Platonists—and among them those of the fifteenth century—developed from certain texts in the Timæus § a doctrine concerning the mystical meaning of hair, which

---

* The purple of Lydda was famous. Compare Fors Clavigera, April, 1876, p. 2, and Deucalion, § 39.

† Pliny, Hist. Nat., VIII. 39.

‡ Under the name of Salacia and Venilia. See St. August., Civ. Dei, VII. 22.

§ Plato, Tim., 75, 76.

coincides with its significance to the vision of early (pre-
Platonic) Greeks. As a tree has its roots in earth, and
set thus, must patiently abide, bearing such fruit as the
laws of nature may appoint, so man, being of other family—these dreamers belonged to a very "pre-scientific
epoch"—has his roots in heaven, and has the power of
moving to and fro over the earth for service to the Law
of Heaven, and as sign of his free descent. Of these
diviner roots the hair is visible type. Plato tells us,* that
of innocent, light-hearted men, "whose thoughts were
turned heavenward," but "who imagined in their simplicity that the clearest demonstration of things above
was to be obtained by sight" the race of birds had being,
by change of external shape into due harmony with the
soul ("μετερρυθμίζετο")—such persons growing feathers
instead of hair.† We have in Dante,‡ too, an inversion
of tree nature parallel to that of the head here. The
tree, with roots in air, whose sweet fruit is, in Purgatory,
alternately, to gluttonous souls, temptation, and purifying
punishment—watered, Landino interprets, by the descending spray of Lethe—signifies that these souls have forgotten the source and limits of earthly pleasure, seeking
vainly in it satisfaction for the hungry and immortal
spirit. So here, this blackened head of the sensual sinner
is rooted to earth, the sign of strength drawn from above
is stripped from off it, and beside it on the sand are laid,
as in hideous mockery, the feet that might have been

---

*Plato, Tim., 91, D. E.

† The most devoid of wisdom were stretched on earth, becoming foot-
less and creeping things, or sunk as fish in the sea. So, we saw Venus'
chosen transmigration was into the form of an eel—other authorities
say, of a fish.

‡ Dante, Purg., XXII., XXIII.

8*

beautiful upon the mountains. Think of the woman's body beyond, and **then of** this head—" instead of 'a girdle, a rent ; and **instead** of well-set hair, baldness." The worm's brethren, the Dragon's elect, wear such shameful tonsure, unencircled **by the** symbolic crown ; prodigal of **life,** " risurgeranno," from no quiet grave, but from this haunt of **horror,** " co crin mozzi " *—in piteous witness of wealth ruinously cast away. Then compare, in **light of** the quotation from Plato above, the dragon's thorny plumage ; compare, too, the charger's mane and tail, and the rippling glory that crowns St. **George.** It is worth while, too, to have in mind the words of the " black cherub " that had overheard the treacherous counsel of Guido de Montefeltro. From the **moment it** was uttered, to that of the sinner's death, the evil spirit says, " stato gli sono a crini " † —lord of his fate. Further, in a Venetian series of engravings illustrating **Dante** (published 1491), the firebreathings of **the Dragon** on Cacus' shoulders transform themselves **into the Centaur's** femininely flowing hair, to signify the inspiration of his forceful fraud. This " power on **his head** " he has because of such an angel.‡ When we consider the **Princess** we shall find this symbolism yet further **carried, but just** now have to notice how the **closely** connected **franchise** of graceful motion, lost to those dishonoured **ones,** is marked by the most carefully-painted **bones** lying on the left—a thigh-bone dislocated from that of the hip, and then thrust **through it.** **Curiously, too, such dislocation would in life produce** a hump, mimicking fairly enough in helpless distor-

---

* Dante, Inf., VII. 57. Purg., XXII. 46.
† Dante, Inf., XXVII.
‡ *Ibid.* XXV.

tion that one to which the frog's leaping power s
due.*

Centrally in the foreground is set the skull, perhaps of
an ape, but more probably of an ape-like man, "with forehead villanous low." This lies so that its eye-socket looks
out, as it were, through the empty eyehole of a sheep's
skull beside it. When man's vision has become ovine
merely, it shall at last, even of grass, see only such bitter
and dangerous growth as our husbandman must reap with
a spear from a dragon's wing.

The remaining minor words of this poem in a forgotten
tongue I cannot definitely interpret. The single skull
with jaw-bone broken off, lying under the dragon's belly,
falls to be mentioned afterwards. The ghastly heap of
them, crowned by a human mummy, withered and
brown,† beside the coil of the dragon's tail, seem meant
merely to add general emphasis to the whole. The
mummy (and not this alone in the picture) may be compared with Spenser's description of the Captain of the
Army of Lusts:—

> " His body lean and meagre as a rake,
> And skin all withered like a dryed rook,
> Thereto as cold and dreary as a snake.
>
> *   *   *   *   *
>
> Upon his head he wore a helmet light,
> Made of a dead man's skull, that seemed a ghastly sight."

The row of five palm trees behind the dragon's head
perhaps refers to the kinds of temptation over which Vic-

---

* 'Ariadne Florentina,' Lect. III., p. 93.

† The venom of the stellio, a spotted species of lizard, emblem of
shamelessness, was held to cause blackening of the face.

tory must be gained, and may thus be illustrated by the
five troops that in Spenser assail the several senses, or beside Chaucer's five fingers of the hand of lust. It may
be observed that Pliny speaks of the Essenes—preceders
of the Christian Hermits—who had given up the world
and its joys as " gens socia palmarum." *

Behind the dragon, in the far background, is a great
city. Its walls and towers are crowded by anxious spectators of the battle. There stands in it, on a lofty pedestal, the equestrian statue of an emperor on horseback, perhaps placed there by Carpaccio for sign of Alexandria,
perhaps merely from a Venetian's pride and joy in the
great figure of Colleone recently set up in his city. In
the background of the opposite (St. George's) side of the
picture rises a precipitous hill, crowned by a church. The
cliffs are waveworn, an arm of the sea passing between
them and the city.

Of these hieroglyphics, only the figure of the princess
now remains for our reading. The expression on her face,
ineffable by descriptive words,† is translated into more
tangible symbols by the gesture of her hands and arms.
These repeat, with added grace and infinitely deepened
meaning, the movement of maidens who encourage The-
seus or Cadmus in their battle with monsters on many
a Greek·vase. They have been clasped in agony and

---

* Pliny, Hist. Nat., V. 17.

† Suppose Caliban had conquered Prospero, and fettered him in a fig-
tree or elsewhere ; that Miranda, after watching the struggle from the
cave, had seen him coming triumphantly to seize her ; and that the first
appearance of Ferdinand is, just at that moment, to her rescue. If we
conceive how she would have looked then, it may give some parallel to
the expression on the princess's face in this picture, but without a certain light of patient devotion here well marked.

prayer, but are now parting—still just a little **doubtfully**
—into a gesture of joyous gratitude to this captain of the
army of salvation and to the captain's Captain. Raphael *
has painted her running from the scene **of** battle. Even
with Tintoret † she turns away for flight; **and if** her hands
are raised to heaven, and her knees fall to the earth, it is
more that she stumbles in a woman's weakness, than that
she abides in faith or sweet self-surrender. Tintoret sees
the scene as in the **first place** a matter of fact, and paints
accordingly, following his judgment of girl nature.‡ Carpaccio sees **it as above** all things a matter of faith, and
paints mythically for our teaching. Indeed, doing this,
he repeats the old legend with more literal accuracy. The
princess was offered as a sacrifice **for** her people. If not
willing, she was at least submissive; nor for herself did
she dream of flight. No chains in the rock were required
for the Christian Andromeda.

"And the king said, . . . 'Daughter, I would you had
died long ago rather than that I should **lose** you thus.'
And she fell at his feet, asking of him a father's blessing.
And when **he had** blessed her once and again, with tears
she went her **way to the shore. Now** St. George chanced
to pass by that place, and he saw her, and asked why she
wept. But she answered, 'Good youth, mount quickly
and flee away, that you die not here shamefully with me.'
Then St. **George said,** 'Fear not, maiden, but tell me what

* Louvre.
† National Gallery.
‡ And perhaps from a certain **ascetic** feeling, a sense growing with
the growing license of Venice, that the soul must rather escape from
this monster by flight, than hope to see it subdued and made serviceable,
(vide p. 10).

it is you wait for here, and all the people stand far off
beholding.'   And she said, ' I see, good youth, how great
of heart you are; but why do you wish to die with me?'
And St. George answered, ' Maiden, do not fear; I go not
hence till you tell me why you weep.'   And when she
had told him all, he answered, ' Maiden, have no fear, for
in the name of Christ will I save you.'   And she said,
' Good soldier,—lest you perish with me!   For that I
perish alone is enough, and you could not save me; you
would perish with me.'   Now while she spoke the dragon
raised his head from the waters.   And the maiden cried
out, all trembling, ' Flee, good my lord, flee away swiftly.' " *   But our " very loyal chevalier of the faith " saw
cause to disobey the lady.

Yet Carpaccio means to do much more than just repeat
this story.   His princess, (it is impossible, without undue
dividing of its substance, to put into logical words the
truth here " embodied in a tale,")—but this princess represents the soul of man.   And therefore she wears a coronet of seven gems, for the seven virtues; and of these,
the midmost that crowns her forehead is shaped into the
figure of a cross, signifying faith, the saving virtue.†   We
shall see that in the picture of Gethsemane also, Carpaccio
makes the representative of faith central.   Without faith,
men indeed may shun the deepest abyss, yet cannot attain
the glory of heavenly hope and love.   Dante saw how
such men—even the best—may not know the joy that is
perfect.   Moving in the divided splendour merely of

---

* Legenda Aurea.

† St. Thomas Aquinas, putting logically the apostle's " substance of
things hoped for," defines faith as " a habit of mind by which eternal
life is begun in us " (Summa II. III. IV. 1).

under earth, on sward whose " fresh verdure," eternally
changeless, expects neither in patient waiting nor in sacred
hope the early and the latter rain,* " Sembianza avevan
nè trista nè lieta."

This maiden, then, is an incarnation **of** spiritual life,
mystically crowned with all the virtues. But their diviner
meaning is yet unrevealed, and following the one legible
command she goes down to such a death for her people,
vainly. Only by help of the hero who slays monstrous
births of nature, **to** sow and tend in its organic **growth**
the wholesome **plant** of civil life, **may she** enter into **that**
liberty **with which** Christ makes His people **free.**

The coronet of the princess is clasped about a close red
cap which hides her hair. **Its** tresses are not yet cast loose,
inasmuch as, till the dragon be subdued, heavenly life is
not secure for the soul, nor its marriage with the great
Bridegroom complete. In corners even of Western Europe
to this day, a maiden's **hair is** jealously covered till her
wedding. Compare **now this head with that** of St. George.
Carpaccio, painting **a divine service of** mute **prayer** and
acted prophecy, **has followed St. Paul's** law concerning
vestments. But **we shall see** how, when prayer is answered and prophecy fulfilled, the long hair—" a glory to
her," and given by Nature for a veil—is sufficient cover-
ing upon the maiden's head, bent in a more mystic rite.

---

* Epistle of James, v., Dante selects (and Carpaccio follows him) as
heavenly judge of **a** right hope that **apostle** who reminds his reader how
man's life is **even** as a vapour that appeareth for a little time and then
vanisheth away. For the connection—geologically historic—of grass
and showers with true human life, compare Genesis ii. 5—8, where the
right translation is, " And no plant of the field was yet in the earth,
and no herb yet sprung up or grown," **etc.**

From the cap hangs a long scarf-like veil. It is twisted
once about the princess's left arm, and then floats in the
air. The effect of this veil strikes one on the first glance
at the picture. It gives force to the impression of natural
fear, yet strangely, in light fold, adds a secret sense of security, as though the gauze were some sacred ægis. And
such indeed it is, nor seen first by Carpaccio, though probably his intuitive invention here. There is a Greek vase-
picture * of Cadmus attacking a dragon, Ares-begotten,
that guarded the sacred spring of the warrior-god. That
fight was thus for the same holy element whose symbolic
sprinkling is the end of this one here. A maiden anx-
iously watches the event ; her gesture resembles the princess's ; her arm is similarly shielded by a fold of her
mantle. But we have a parallel at once more familiar
and more instructively perfect than this. Cadmus had a
daughter, to whom was given power upon the sea, because
in utmost need she had trusted herself to the mercy of its
billows. Lady of its foam, in hours when "the blackening
wave is edged with white," she is a holier and more helpful Aphrodite,—a "water-sprite" whose voice foretells
that not "wreck" but salvation "is nigh." In the last
and most terrible crisis of that long battle with the Power
of Ocean, who denied him a return to his Fatherland,
Ulysses would have perished in the waters without the
veil of Leucothea wrapped about his breast as divine life-
buoy. And that veil, the "immortal" $\varkappa\rho\acute{\eta}\delta\epsilon\mu\nu\sigma\nu$,† was

---

* Inghirami gives this (No. 239).

† In pursuance of the same symbolism, Troy walls were once literally
called "salvation," this word, with, for certain historical reasons, the
added epithet of "holy," being applied to them. With the $\varkappa\rho\eta\delta\epsilon\mu\nu\alpha$
Penelope shielded her "tender" cheeks in presence of the suitors.

just such a scarf attached to the head-dress as this one of
the princess's here.* Curiously, too, we shall see that
Leucothea (at first called Ino), of Thebes' and Cadmus'
line, daughter of Harmonia, is closely connected with certain sources of the story of St. George.† But we have
first to consider the dragon's service.

* Vide Nitsch ad Od., **V. 346.**

† λεγοντι δ' εν και θαλάσσα
. . . βιοτον άφθιτον
Ἰνοῖ τετάχθαι τὸν ὅλον ἀμφὶ χρόνον.

(Pind. Ol., II. 51.)

The Editor had hope of publishing this book a full year
ago. He now in all humility, yet not in uncertainty, can
sum the causes of its delay, both with respect to his friend
and to himself, in the words of St. Paul,

και ενέκοψεν ήμας ό Σατανᾶς.

BRANTWOOD,
6th March, 1879.

APPENDIX TO CHAPTER VIII.

SANCTUS, SANCTUS, SANCTUS.

AN ACCOUNT OF THE MOSAICS IN THE BAPTISTERY OF ST. MARK'S.

" The whole edifice is to be regarded less as a temple wherein to pray than as itself a Book of Common Prayer, a vast illuminated missal, bound with alabaster instead of parchment."

Stones of **Venice,** ii. 4, 46.

" We must take some pains, therefore, when we enter St. Mark's, to read all that is inscribed, or we shall not penetrate into the feeling either of the builder or of his times." *Stones of Venice,* ii. 4, 64.

THE following catalogue of the mosaics of the Baptistery of St. Mark's was written in the autumn of 1882, after a first visit to Venice, and was then sent to Mr. Ruskin as a contribution to his collected records of the church. It was not intended for publication, but merely as notes or material for which he might possibly find some use ; and if the reader in Venice will further remember that it is the work of no artist or antiquarian, but of a traveller on his holiday, he will, it is hoped, be the more ready to pardon errors and omissions which his own observation can correct and supply. The mosaics of the Baptistery are, of course, only a small portion of those to be seen throughout the church, but that portion is one complete in itself, and more than enough to illustrate the vast amount of thought contained in the scripture legible on the walls of

St. Mark's by every comer who is desirous of taking any real interest in the building.

The reader, then, who proposes to make use of the present guide can, by reference to the following list, see at a glance the subjects with which these mosaics deal, and the order in which his attention will be directed to them. They are, in addition to the altar-piece, these:—

  I. The Life of St. John the Baptist.
  II. The Infancy of Christ.
  III. St. Nicholas.
  IV. The Four Evangelists.
  V. The Four Saints.
  VI. The Greek Fathers.
  VII. The Latin Fathers.
 VIII. Christ and the Prophets.
  IX. Christ and the Apostles.
  X. Christ and the Angels.

The subject of the altar-piece is the Crucifixion. In the centre is Christ on the cross, with the letters $\overline{\text{IC}}$. $\overline{\text{XC}}$. on either side. Over the cross are two angels, veiling their faces with their robes; at its foot lies a skull,—Golgotha, —upon which falls the blood from Christ's feet, whilst on each side of the Saviour are five figures, those at the extreme ends of the mosaic being a doge and dogaress, probably the donors of the mosaic.

To the left is St. Mark—S $\overline{\text{MARCVS}}$—with an open book in his hand, showing the words, "In illo tempore Maria mater. . . ." "In that hour Mary his mother...." She stands next the cross, with her hands clasp in grief; above her are the letters M—P Θ V—$\mu\eta\tau\tilde{\eta}\rho$ $\Theta\epsilon o\tilde{v}$—Mother of God.

To the right of the cross is St. John the Evangelist—S. IOHES EVG—his face covered with his hands, receiving charge of the Virgin: "When Jesus, therefore, saw his mother, and the disciple standing by, whom he loved, he saith unto his mother, Woman, behold thy son! Then saith he to the disciple, Behold thy mother! And from that hour the disciple took her unto his own home" (St. John xix. 26, 27).

Lastly, next St. John the Evangelist is St. John the Baptist, bearing a scroll, on which are the words:

"ECCE AGNUS DEI ECE...."

"Ecce agnus Dei, ecce qui tollit peccatum mundi."

"Behold the Lamb of God which taketh away the sin of the world" (St. John i. 29).*

I. THE LIFE OF ST. JOHN THE BAPTIST.—Leaving the altar and turning to the right, we have the first mosaic in the series which gives the life of the Baptist, and consists in all of ten pictures.   (See opposite plan.)

a. His birth is announced.

b. He is born and named.

c. He is led into the desert.

d. He receives a cloak from an angel.

e. He preaches to the people.

---

* The scriptural references in this appendix are, first, to the Vulgate, which most of the legends in the Baptistery follow, and, secondly, to the English version of the Bible. The visitor will also notice that throughout the chapel the scrolls are constantly treated by the mosaicists literally as scrolls, the text being cut short even in the middle of a word by the curl of the supposed parchment.

PLAN OF THE BAPTISTERY.

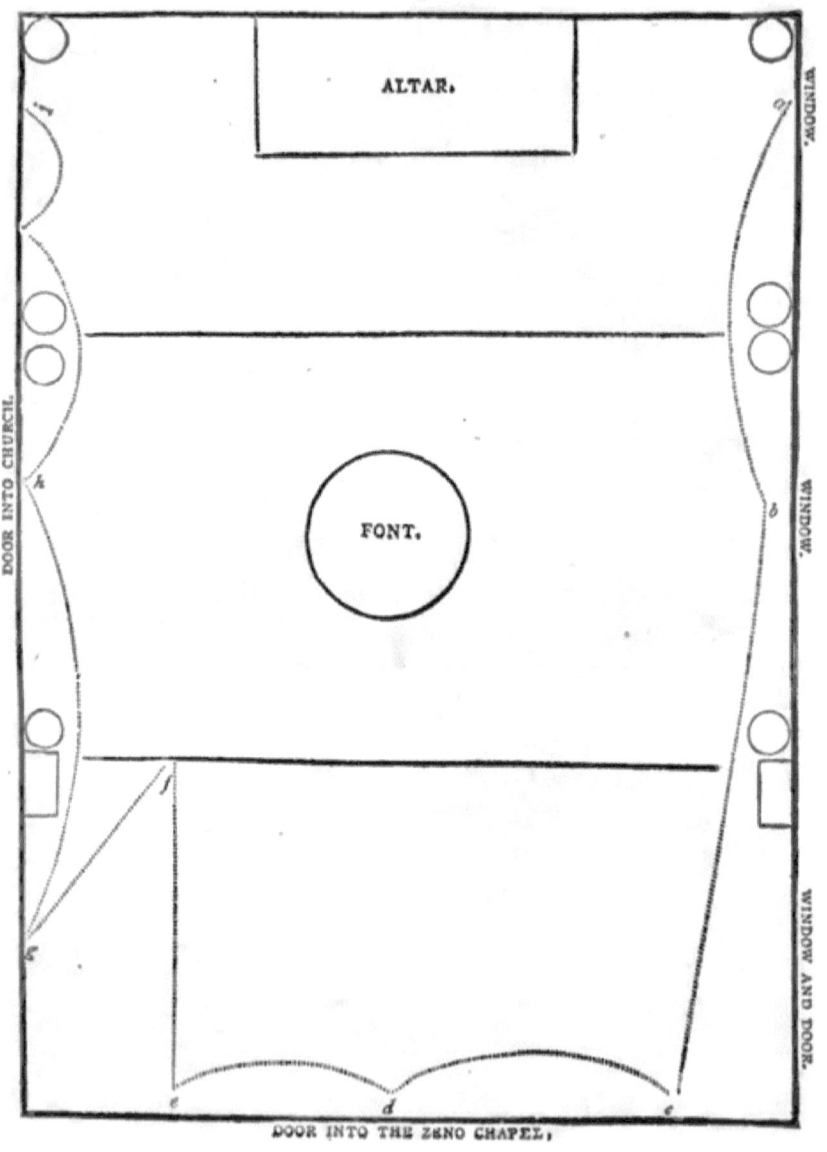

f. He answers the Pharisees.

g. He baptizes Christ.

h. He is condemned to death.　　　/

i. He is beheaded.

j. He is buried.

a. His birth is announced.—This mosaic has three divisions.

1. To the left is Zacharias at the altar, with the angel appearing to him. He swings a censer, burning incense "in the order of his course." He has heard the angel's message, for his look and gesture show clearly that he is already struck dumb. Above are the words:

INGRESSO ZACHARIA TĒPLV̄ DN̄I
APARVIT EI AGLS̄ DN̄I STĀS
A DEXTRIS ALTARIS

" Ingresso Zacharia templum domini aparuit ei angelus domini stans a dextris altaris."

" When Zacharias had entered the temple of the Lord there appeared to him an angel of the Lord standing on the right side of the altar " (St. Luke i. 9–11).

2. " And the people waited for Zacharias, and marvelled that he tarried so long in the temple. And when he came out, he could not speak unto them: and they perceived that he had seen a vision in the temple: for he beckoned unto them, and remained speechless " (St. Luke i. 21 22).

✠ H. S. ZAHARIAS EXIT
TUTUS AD PP̄LM

" Hic sanctus Zacharias exit tutus ad populum."

" Here saint Zacharias comes out safe to the people."

9

3. "He departed to his own house" (St. Luke i. 23). Zacharias embracing his wife Elizabeth.

✠ S̄. ZAIA
RIAS. S̄. ELI
SABETA

b. He is born and named (opposite the door into the church).—Zacharias is seated to the left* of the picture, and has a book or "writing table" in front of him, in which he has written "Johannes est nomen ejus"—"His name is John" (Luke i. 63). To the right an aged woman, Elizabeth, points to the child inquiringly, "**How** would you have him called?"; further to the right, another and younger woman kneels, holding out the child to his father. **At** the back a servant with a basket in her arms looks on. Unlike the other two women, she has no glory about her head. Above is a tablet inscribed :—

NATIVITAS
SANCTI JOHANNIS
BAPTISTÆ

and below another tablet, with the date and artist's name—

FRAN' TURESSIVS V.F. MDCXXVIII.

Turning now to the west wall, and standing with the altar behind us, we have the next three mosaics of the series, thus—

---

* By "right" and "left" in this appendix is meant always the right and left hand of the spectator as he faces his subject.

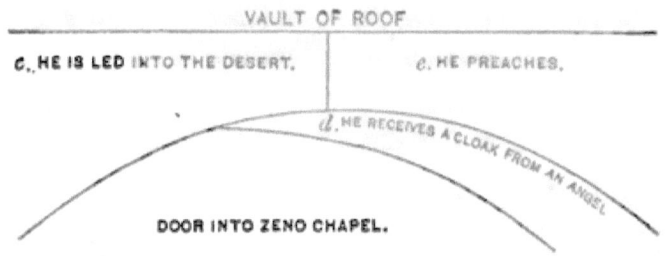

c. *He is led into the* ***desert.***—The words of the legends
are :—

✣ QVOM ANGELV' SEDOVXAT S. IOHAN.
I. DESERTUM.

"Quomodo angelus seduxit (?) sanctum **Johannem**
in desertum."
"**How** an angel led away saint John **into** the desert."

This is not biblical. "And **the child** grew **and** waxed
strong in spirit, and was in the deserts till the day of his
showing unto Israel" **is all** St. Luke (i. 80) **says.** Here
the infant Baptist is being led **by** an angel, who points
onward **with one** hand, and with the other holds that of
the child, who, **so** far from being " strong in spirit," looks
troubled, **and has one hand** placed on his heart in evident
fear. His other **hand, in** the grasp of the angel's, does not
in any **way** hold it, **but is** held by it ; he **is** literally *being*
led into the desert somewhat against his **will.** The word
sedouaxat (? mediæval for seduxit) may here well have this
meaning **of** persuasive leading. It should also be noted
that the child and his guide are already far on their way :
they have left all vegetation behind them ; only a stony
rock and rough ground, **with** one or two tufts of grass and
a leafless tree, are visible.

d. He receives a cloak from an angel.—This is also not biblical. The words above the mosaic are—

HC A͞GELUS REPRESĒTAT VESTE BTO IOHI

" Hic angelus representat vestem **be** to Johanni."
" Here the angel gives (back?) **a** garment to the blessed John."

St. John wears his cloak of camel's hair, and holds in one hand a scroll, on which is written an abbreviation of the Greek " μετανοε̄ιτε "—" Repent ye."

MT
NO
⊿T
E

e. He preaches to the people.

HIC PREDIC͞AT.*

" Here he preaches " [or " predicts the Christ "].

The Baptist is gaunt and thin ; he wears his garment of camel's hair, and has in his hand a staff with a cross at the top of it. He stands in a sort of pulpit, behind which is a building, presumably a church ; whilst in front of him listen three old men, a woman, and a child. Below are three more **women**.

f. He answers the Pharisees (on the wall opposite *e*).— To the right are the priests and Levites sent from Je- rusalem, asking, " What says he of himself ? " They are four in number, a Rabbi and three Pharisees. To the left is St. John with two disciples behind him. Between them rolls the Jordan, at the ferry to which (Bethabara)

---

* The mark of abbreviation over the C shows the omission of an h in the mediæval " predichat."

the discussion between the Baptist and the Jews took place, and across the river the Rabbi asks:

QVÔM . ERGO . BÆPT
ZAS . SI NQE . XPS . NE
Q̃ . HELLA,. NEQ' PHA

" Quomodo ergo baptizas si neque Christus, neque Elia, neque Propheta ? " *
" Why baptizest thou, then, if thou be not that Christ, nor Elias, neither that prophet ? " (John i. 25).

St. John does not, however, give the answer recorded of him in the Gospel, but another written above his head thus :—

✠ EGO BAPTIZO IÑO
MĪE PATRIS
ET . FILII . 7 . S̄P'
S̄C̄I

" Ego baptizo in nomine patrio et filii & Spiritus sancti."
" I baptize in the name of the Father, and Son, and Holy Spirit."

g. He baptizes Christ.

HICE BAPTISMV' XPI

On the left is a tree with an axe laid to its root. In the centre stands St. John, with his hand on the head of Christ, who stands in the midst of the river. Three angels look down from the right bank into the water ; and in it are five fishes, over one of which Christ's hand is raised in blessing. Below is a child with a golden vase in one hand, probably the river god of the Jordan, who is sometimes introduced into these pictures. From above a

* The Vulgate has " Quid ergo baptizas si tu non es," etc.

ray of light, with a star and a dove in it, descends on the
head of Christ: " And Jesus when he was baptized, went
up straightway out of the water: and, lo, the heavens
were opened unto him, and he saw the Spirit of God descending like a dove, and lighting upon him: and lo, a
voice from heaven, saying, This is my beloved Son, in
whom I am well pleased " (Matt. iii. 16, 17).

h. His death is commanded by Herod (over the door
into the main body of the church).

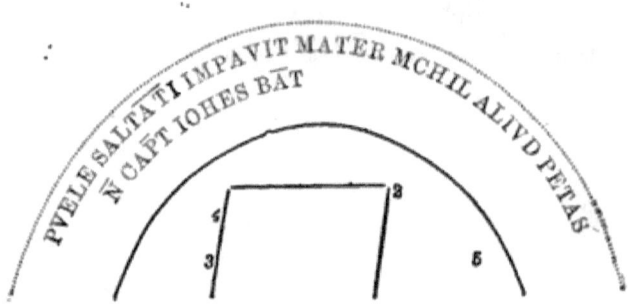

The mosaic is (according to the sacristan) entirely restored,
and the letters of the legend appear to have been incorrectly treated. The words are " Puellæ saltanti impera-
vit mater nihil (? mchil) aliud petas nisi caput Johannis
Baptistæ "—" And as the girl danced her mother commanded her, saying, Ask for nothing else, but only for the
head of John the Baptist."

Five figures are seen in the mosaic :—

1. Herod with his hands raised in horror and distress,
" exceeding sorry " (Mark vi. 26).

2. Herodias, pointing at him, with a smile of triumph.

3. Herodias' daughter dancing, with the charger on her
head.

4. Another figure with regard to which see *ante*, p. 96, § 8, where it is suggested that the figure is St. John at a former time, saying to Herod, " It is not lawful for thee to have her." If this is not **so**, it may be that the **figure** represents the " lords, high captains, **and chief** estates **of** Galilee " (Mark vi. 21) who were at **the feast.**

5. A servant in attendance.

i. He is beheaded.

✠ DECHOLACIO SCI IOHIS BAT.
" **The** beheading of St. John the Baptist."

To the left is the headless body of St. John, still in prison. "And immediately the king sent an executioner (or ' one of his guard '), and he went and beheaded him in prison." The Baptist has leant forward, and his hands are stretched out, as if to save himself in falling. A Roman soldier is sheathing his sword, and looks somewhat disgusted at the daughter of Herodias as she carries the head to her mother, who sits enthroned near. (See *ante*, p. 98, § 10.)

j. He is buried.—" And when his disciples heard of it they came and took up his corpse and laid it in a tomb " (Mark vi. 29).

H. SEPELITVR . CO
RPVS . S . IOHIS . BAT
(See *ante*, p. 98, § 10.)

" Hic sepelitur corpus sancti Johannis Baptistæ "—" Here is being buried the **body of** St. John the Baptist."

The headless body of the Baptist is being laid in the grave by two disciples, whilst a third swings a censer over it.

II. The Infancy of Christ.—Going back now to the

west end of the chapel, we have four mosaics representing scenes in the infancy of Christ.

1. The wise men before Herod. } Above *c* and *e* in the
2. The wise men adoring Christ. } Life of St. John.
3. The flight into Egypt. } Opposite 1 and 2.
4. The Holy Innocents. }

1. *The wise men before Herod.*

Herod is seated on his throne, attended by a Roman soldier; he looks puzzled and anxious. Before him are the three kings in attitudes of supplication ; and above are the words—

✤ VBIE .QVINATU' . EST . REX . JUDÆORUM.

"Ubi est qui natus est rex Judæorum ?" } St. Matt. ii. 2.
"Where is he that is born king of the Jews ?" }

2. *The wise men adoring Christ.*

✤ ADORABVT EV ONS REGES TERE ET OMS GETES SERVIENT EI

"Adorabunt eum omnes reges terræ, (et) omes gentes servient ei."
"Yea, all kings shall fall down before him ; all nations shall serve him " (Psalm lxxii. 10, 11).

In the centre is the Madonna seated on a throne, which is also part of the stable of the inn. On her knees is the infant Christ, with two fingers of his right hand raised in benediction. The Madonna holds out her hand, as if showing the Child to the kings, who approach Him with gifts and in attitudes of devout worship. To the left is a man leading a camel out of a building ; whilst to the right of the stable lies Joseph asleep, with an angel descending to him : " Arise and take the young child." (See the next mosaic.) The rays from the central figure of the vaulted roof fall, one on the second of the three kings, and another, the most brilliant of them,—upon which, where it breaks into triple glory, the star of Bethlehem is set,—upon the Madonna and the Christ.

3. *The flight into Egypt.*

✠ SVRGE ET ACCIPE PUERVM ET MATREM EU' ET FUGE
  IN EGYPTUM ..ET ESTO IBI USQ' DVM DICAM TIBI

"Surge et accipe puerum et matrem ejus et fuge in Egyptum et esto ibi usque dum dicam tibi."

"Arise and take the young child and his mother, and flee into Egypt, and be there until I bring thee word" (St. Matt.ii. 13).

A youth carrying a gourd leads into a building with a mosque-like dome a white ass, on which is seated the Madonna, holding the infant Christ.   Joseph walks behind, carrying a staff and cloak.   The fact of the journey being sudden and hasty is shown by the very few things which the fugitives have taken with them—only a cloak and a gourd; they have left the presents of the three kings behind.

4. *The Holy Innocents.*

✠TUNC . HERODE' VIDE' Q'M ILVSV' EE̅T AMAGI' IRATV'E . RE,
                                         DE . 7 . MIT
TES OCCIDIT.OMS PUERO' QVI. ERANT. BETHLEEM Q̄M .OIRVS
         FINIBUS . EIVS *

"Tunc Herodes videns quoniam illusus esset a magis iratus est valde, et mittens occidit omnes pueros qui erant in Bethlehem et in omnibus finibus ejus."

"Then Herod, when he saw that he was mocked of the wise men, was

* The letters underlined are unintelligible, as otherwise the legend follows the Vulgate.   Possibly the words have been retouched, and the letters incorrectly restored.

9*

exceeding wroth, and sent forth, and slew all the children that were in Bethlehem, and in all the coasts thereof " (Matt. ii. 16).

Three Roman soldiers are killing the children, some of whom already lie dead and bleeding on the rocky ground. To the right is a mother with her child in her arms, and near her another woman is holding up her hands in grief.

III. St. Nicholas.

Just below the mosaic of the Holy Innocents is one of S. NICOLAU'—St. Nicholas—with one hand raised in benediction whilst the other holds a book. He is here, close to the small door that opens on to the Piazzetta, the nearest to the sea of all the saints in St. Mark's, because he is the sea saint, the patron of all ports, and especially of Venice. He was, it is well known, with St. George and St. Mark, one of the three saints who saved Venice from the demon ship in the storm when St. Mark gave to the fishermen the famous ring.

There now remain for the traveller's examination the three vaults of the Baptistery, the arches leading from one division of the chapel to another, and the spandrils which support the font and altar domes. In the arch leading from the west end of the chapel to the front are the four evangelists; in that leading from the dome over the font to that over the altar are four saints, whilst in the spandrils of the two last-named domes are, over the font, the four Greek, and over the altar the four Latin fathers.

IV. The Four Evangelists.

S. LUCAS EVG.

St. Luke is writing in a book, and has written a letter and a half, possibly QV, the first two letters of Quonium

—" Forasmuch "—which is the opening word of his **Gospel.**

S. MARCVS EṼG.

St. Mark is sharpening his pencil, and has a pair of pincers on his desk.

S. IOHES EVG.

St. John is represented as very old,—alluding of course to his having written his Gospel late in life.

S. MATHEV' EVG.

St. Matthew is writing, and just dipping his pen in the ink.

V. FOUR SAINTS—*St. Anthony, St. Pietro Urseolo, St. Isidore, St. Theodore.*

a. St. Anthony (on the left at the bottom of the arch).

" Il beato Antonio di Bresa."

IL B	EA
TO	AN
TON	IO
DI	BR
E	SA

St. Anthony is the hermit saint. He stands here with clasped hands, and at his side is a skull, the sign of penitence. He wears, as in many other pictures of him, a monk's dress, in allusion to his being " the founder of ascetic monachism." " His temptations" are well known.

b. St. Pietro Urseolo (above St. Anthony).

" Beatus Petrus Ursiolo dux(s) Vened."
" The blessed Pietro Urseolo, Doge of the Venetians."

✚ BEA	TUS
PETER	V'VRSI
O	DUXS
LO	VENED

This Doge turned monk. Influenced by the teaching of the abbot Guarino, when he came to Venice from his convent in Guyenne, Pietro left his ducal palace one September night, fled from Venice, and shut himself up in the monastery of Cusano, where he remained for nineteen years, till his death in 997.

Here he is represented as a monk in a white robe, with a black cloak. He holds in his hand the Doge's cap, which he has doffed for ever, and as he looks upwards, there shines down on him a ray of light, in the centre of which is seen the Holy Dove.

c. St. Isidore (opposite the Doge).

S. ISIDORVS MARTIR (?)

This is St. Isidore of Chios, a martyr saint, who perished during the persecutions of the Christians by the Emperor Decius, A.D. 250. He appears to have been much worshipped at Venice, where he is buried. Here he is seen dressed as a warrior, and bearing a shield and a lily, the symbol of purity.*

d. St. Theodore. s. THEODOR. M.

He is with St. George, St. Demetrius, and St. Mercurius, one of the four Greek warrior saints of Christendom, besides being, of course, the patron saint of Venice. He is martyr as well as warrior, having fired the temple of Cybele, and perished in the flames, A.D. 300.

The four saints upon this arch thus represent two forms of Christian service; St. Anthony and the Doge being

---

* See *Stones of Venice*, vol. ii. chap. viii. § 127, and vol. iii. chap. ii. § 61. His body was brought to Venice with that of St. Donato in 1126 by the Doge Domenico Michiel. See *ante*, p. 11.

chosen as types of asceticism, and the other two as examples of actual martyrdom.

VI. THE FOUR GREEK FATHERS—*St. John Chrysostom, St. Gregory Nazianzenus, St. Basil the Great, and St. Athanasius* (on the spandrils of the central dome).

a. S. IOHES CRISOSTOMOS PATKA (patriarch), on the right of the door leading into the church.

He has no mitre, being one of the Greek Fathers, who are thus distinguished from the Latin Fathers, all of whom, except St. Jerome (the cardinal), wear mitres.

He bears a scroll—

   ✠ REG
   NVM.I
   NTRA   "Regnum intrabit, quem non sit
   BIT.Q   purus arte lavabit."
   VE.NON   "He shall enter the kingdom : who
   S.PVR   is not clean, him shall he thoroughly
   VS ÆRT   wash."
   E.LAV
   ABIT

b. S. GREGORIVS NAZIANZENVS (to the right of St. John Chrysostom). He is represented, as he usually is, as old and worn with fasting. On his scroll is written—

   ✠ QVO
   DNA
   TVRA   "Quod natura tulit Christus baptis-
   TVLI   mate curat.
   T XPS   "What nature has brought, Christ
   BAPTI   by baptism cures."
   SMAT
   ECV
   RAT

c. S. BASIL (to the right of his friend St. Gregory). St. Basil the Great, the founder of monachism in the East, began his life of devotion in early youth, and is here represented as a young man. The order of the Basilicans is still the only order in the Greek Church. His scroll has—

✛ UT SO
LE EST
PRIMUM
LUX)MU
RIRIDE
BATIS
MUM

"Ut sole est primum lux" (as by the sun first we have light). The rest is unintelligible, except the last word, which suggests that the comparison is between the light of the sun and the spiritual light of baptism.

d. S. ATHANASIUS, old and white-haired. His scroll runs—

✛ UT UN
UM EST
NUM
EN SI
C SACR
NERE
OMU
ALV
MEN

"Ut unum est numen, sic sacro munere *a lumen* (? atque lumen)."

"As the Godhead is one, so also by God's gift is light" (?)

VII. THE FOUR LATIN FATHERS—*St. Jerome, St. Ambrose, St. Augustine, and St. Gregory the Great* (on the spandrils of the altar dome).

The light here is very bad; and even after accustoming himself to it, the reader will hardly be able to do more than see that all four figures have books before them, in which they are writing, apparently in Greek characters.

What they have written—in no case more than a few letters—is impossible to decipher from the floor of the chapel. St. Jerome wears his cardinal's hat and robes, and St. Ambrose has his bee-hive near him, in allusion to the story that when in his cradle a swarm of bees once lighted on his lips and did not sting him.

The visitor has thus examined all the mosaics except those of the three domes. He must now, therefore, return from near the altar to the further end of the chapel, and take first the vaulting (for accurately this is not a dome) of that part of the roof.

VIII. Christ and the Prophets.

In the centre is Christ, surrounded by the prophets and patriarchs of the Old Testament, each of whom unfolds a scroll and displays on it a portion of his own prophecy.

Standing with his back to the altar, the visitor will thus see to the left of the Christ, Zephaniah and Elisha, and to his right Isaiah and Hosea.

1. *ZEPHANIAH.* SOPHONIAH PHA (propheta).

His scroll runs thus :—

EXPE	"Expecta me in die resurrectionis
TA ME	mere quoniam ju(dicium meum ut
IN DIE	congregem gentes)."
RESU	See Zeph. iii. 8. This legend. is
RECT	shortened, and not quite accurately
IONIS	quoted, from the Vulgate. Our ver-
MEE	sion is :—
QUO	"Wait ye upon me until the day
NIMA	that I rise up . . . for my determina-
IU	tion is to gather the nations. . . ."

2. *ELISHA.*   ELISEAS PĨA

    Scroll :— PATER
         MI PA   " Pater mi, pater mi, currus Israel
         TER MI   et auriga ejus."
         CURRU'   " My father, my father, the chariot
         ISRAEL   of Israel and the horsemen thereof."
         ETAU   2 Kings ii. 12.
         RIGA
         EIVS

3. *ISAIAH.*   ISAIAS
                  PĨA

    Scroll :—ECCE V   " Ecce virgo concipiet et pariet fil-
         IRGOc   ium et vocabitur nom (en ejus Emman-
         CIPIET   uel)."
         ET PAR   " Behold a-virgin shall conceive and
         IET FILI   bear a son, and shall call his name Im-
         UM ET V   manuel." *
         OCABIT   Isa. vii. 14.
         UR NOM̄

4. *HOSEA.*   OSIA
                  PĨA

    Scroll :—VENIT
         EET. RE   " Venite et revertamur ad dominum
         VERTA   quia ipse cepit et sana (bit nos)."
         MURAD   " Come and let us return unto the
         DOMINŪ   Lord, for he has torn and he will heal
         QVIA   us."
         IPSE CE   Hosea vi. 1.
         PIT ET
         SANA

Then turning around and facing the altar, we have, to the

* Isaiah is constantly represented with these words on his scroll, as, for example, on the roof of the Arena Chapel at Padua, and on the western porches of the cathedral of Verona.

left of the Christ, Jeremiah and Elijah ; to the right, Abraham and Joel.

5. *JEREMIAH.*

JEREMIAS
PĨA

Scroll :—HIC EST
DEVS
NOSTER
ET NON
EXTIMA
BITUR
ALIVS

" Hic est Deus noster et **non extima-**
bitur alius."
" This is our **God, and none** other
shall be feared."

6. *ELIJAH.*

ELIA
PĨA

Scroll :—DOMIN
ESICO
NUER
SUS
AVEN
IT **PO**
PVLVS
TV
VS

" Domine si(c) conversus avenit **pop-**
ulus **tuus.**"
"**Lord, thus are thy people como**
against thee.**"
This is **not** biblical.   It is noticeable that **Elijah,** unlike the other
prophets, **who look** at the spectator,
is turning **to** the Christ, whom he
addresses.

7. *ABRAHAM.*

ABRAN
PĨA

Scroll :—VISITA
VIT DO
MINUS
SARAM
SICUT
PROMI
SERAT

" Visitavit **(autem)** dominus Saram
sicut promiserat."
" The Lord visited Sarah as he had
said."

Gen. xxi. 1.

8. *JOEL.*

                     JOEL
                     P̃HA

Scroll :—SUPER
        SERVO(S)   "Super servos meos et super ancillas
        MEOSET   effundam de spiritu meo." *
        SUPERA   "Upon my men servants and hand-
        NCILAS   maids will I pour out (of) my spirit."
        ERUNEA   Joel ii. 29.
        MDES
        PVMEO

Then, still facing the altar, there are on the wall to the right David and Solomon; on that to the left, above the Baptism of Christ, Obadiah and Jonah.

9. *DAVID.*

                     DAVID
                     P̃HA

Scroll :—FILIUS
        MEV.E   "Filius meus es tu, ego hodie genui
        STŪ.E   te."
        GO.II   "Thou art my son, this day have I
        ODIE   begotten thee."
        GEN   Psalm ii. 7.
        UI.T
        E

10. *SOLOMON.*

                     SALOMON
                     P̃HA

Scroll :—QVESI
        VI.ILLV
        M.ETNO   "Quæsivi illum et non inveni-inven-
        NINVEN   erunt in me vigiles qui custodiunt
        I.IŪENE   civitatem."
        RŪT.IN   "I sought him, but I found him not.
        ME.VIGI   The watchmen that go about the city
        LE.QVI   found (or 'came upon') me."
        CUTO   Song of Solomon, iii. 2, 3.
        DIUT
        CIUI
        TA
        TEM

---

* The mosaic has apparently "erundam" for "effundam," possibly a restorer's error. The Vulgate has "spiritum neum," for "de spiritu meo."

11. *OBADIAH.*

ABDIAS
PH̄A

Scroll :—ECCE
　　　PARV
　　　ULVM
　　　DEDI
　　　TTE
　　　INGE
　　　NTI
　　　BV
　　　S

　　" Ecce parvulum dedit te in gen-
tibus."
　　" Behold he has made thee small
among the heathen."
　　　　　　　　　　　Obadiah 2.
　　(Vulgate has " dedi : " and so has
our Bible " I have.")

12. *JONAH.*

JONAS
PH̄A

Scroll :—CLAMA
　　　VIADD
　　　OMINU
　　　MEEX
　　　AUDI
　　　VITME
　　　DETR
　　　IBULA
　　　MEA. TIO
　　　　　N̄

　　" Clamavi ad dominum et exaudivit
me de tribulation mea."
　　" I cried by reason of my affliction
to the Lord, and he heard me."
　　　　　　　　　　Jonah ii. 2.

IX. CHRIST AND THE APOSTLES.　(See *ante*, p. 95. § 8.)
Passing now to under the central dome, Christ is again
seen enthroned in the midst, no longer, however, of the
prophets, but of his own disciples.　He is no longer the
Messiah, but the risen Christ.　He wears gold and red, the
emblems of royalty ; his right hand is raised in blessing;
his left holds the resurrection banner and a scroll.　The
marks of the nails are visible in the hands and feet here
only ; they are not to be seen, of course, in the previous
vaulting, nor are they in the third or altar dome where he
sits enthroned triumphant as the Heavenly King.

Scroll :—EVNTES
      INMV̄DV̄
      UNIVES
      VM.PRE
      DICHAT
      EEVAN
      GELIV
      MOMIC
      REATU
      REQI
      CRĒDI
      DERI
      TEBA
      PTIS
      ATU

"Euntes in· mundum universum prædicate evangelium omni creaturæ. Qui crediderit et baptizatu(s fuerit salvus erit)."

"Go ye into all the world, and preach the Gospel to every creature. He that believeth and is baptized shall be saved."

St. Mark xvi. 15, 16.

Below, right round the dome, are the twelve Apostles, baptizing each in the country with which his ministry is actually or by tradition most associated. A list of them has been already given (*ante*, p. 96, § 8), with their countries, except that of St. Bartholomew, which is there noted as "indecipherable." It is, however, legible as India.

Each Apostle is the centre of a similar group, consisting of the Apostle himself, his convert, in the moment of baptism, and a third figure whose position is doubtful. He may be awaiting baptism, already baptized, or merely an attendant: in the group of St. James the Less, he holds a towel; in that of St. Thomas, a cross; and in every case he wears the costume of the country where the baptism is taking place. Thus, to take the most striking instances, St. Philip's Phrygian has the red Phrygian cap; St. Peter's Roman is a Roman soldier; the Indians of St. Thomas and St. Bartholemew are (except for some slight variety of color) both dressed alike, and wear turbans. Behind the figures is in each group a building, also characteristic

architecturally of the given country. In two instances
there is seen a tree growing out of this building, namely,
in the case of Palestine and in that of Achaia; but whether
or no with any special meaning or allusion may be doubtful.

The inscriptions are as follows (see *ante*, **p. 96**):

SCS IOHES EVG BAPTIZA	I EFESO
S. IACOB MINOR . . .	I JUDEA
S. PHVLIP	I FRIGIA
S. MATHEV'	I ETHOPIA
S. SIMEON	I EGIPTV
S. TOMAS	IN INDIA
S. ANDRE	I ACHAIA
S. PETRV'	IN ROMA
S. BARTOLOMEV' . .	I INDIA
S. TADEV'	I MESOPOTAMIA
S. MATIAS	I PALESTIN
SCS MARCTS·EVS . .	I ALESANDRIA

In this list, most careful reference is made, as has been
said, to the various traditions concerning the places of each
Apostle's special ministry, the main tradition being always
followed in cases of doubt. Thus St. John was bishop
of Ephesus; St. James the Less bishop of Jerusalem, where
he received St. Paul, and introduced him to the Church;
St. Philip labored in Phrygia, and is said to have died
at Hierapolis; St. Matthew chiefly in Ethiopia; St. Simeon
in Egypt; and St. Thomas (though this may be by confusion with another Thomas) is said to have preached in
India and founded the Church at Malabar, where his tomb
is shown, and "Christians of St. Thomas" is still a name
for the Church. So, again, St. Andrew preached in Achaia,
and was there crucified at Patræ; the connection of St.
Peter with Rome needs no comment; both Jerome and

Eusebius assign India to St. Bartholomew; St. Thaddæus or Jude preached in Syria and Arabia, and died at Eddessa; the first fifteen years of the ministry of St. Matias were spent in Palestine; and lastly, St. Mark is reported to have been sent by St. Peter to Egypt, and there founded the Church at Alexandria.

X. CHRIST AND THE ANGELS.

We pass lastly to the altar-dome, already partly described in the " Requiem " chapter of this book (p. 96 § 9).

In the centre is Christ triumphant, enthroned on the stars, with the letters $\overline{IC}$ $\overline{XC}$ once more on either side of him. In the circle with him are two angels, whose wings veil all but their faces; round it are nine other angels, ruby-colored for love, and bearing flaming torches. "He maketh his angels spirits, and his ministers a flaming fire."

Lower down round the dome are the "angels and archangels and all the company of heaven," who "laud and magnify His glorious name." These heavenly agencies are divided into three hierarchies, each of three choirs, and these nine choirs are given round this vault.

Hierarchy I.` . . . Seraphim, Cherubim, Thrones.
Hierarchy II. . . . Dominations, Virtues, Powers.
Hierarchy III . . . Princedoms, Archangels, Angels.

" The first three choirs receive their glory immediately from God, and transmit it to the second; the second illuminate the third; the third are placed in relation to the created universe and man. The first hierarchy are as councillors; the second as governors; the third as ministers. The Seraphim are absorbed in perpetual love and adoration immediately round the throne of God; the Cherubim know and worship; the Thrones sustain the seat of the **Most High.** The Dominations, Virtues, Powers, are the regents of the stars and elements. The last three orders—Princedoms, Archangels, and Angels—are the protectors of the great monarchies on earth, and the executors of the will of God throughout the universe." *

The visitor can see for himself how accurately this statement is borne out by the mosaics of the altar-dome. Immediately over the altar, and **nearest** therefore to the presence of God, is the Cherubim, "the Lord of those that know," with the words "fulness of knowledge," "plenitudo scientiæ," on his heart; to **the** left is the Seraphim; to the right the Thrones, "sustaining the seat of the Most High." Further to the right come the Dominations—an armed angel, holding in one hand a balance, in the other a spear. In one scale of the balance **is** a man, in the other the book of the law; and this latter scale is being just snatched at by a winged demon, **who,** grovelling on **the ground, turns** round to meet the spear of **the** angel. Opposite the Dominations are the Princedoms **or** Principalities, **another** armed angel, wearing a helmet and calmly seated **among the** stars; and the Powers (" **potestates**") with a black **devil** chained **at** his feet. The Virtues come next, **with** a skeleton **in a** grave below, and **at the** back a pillar of **fire**; and, **lastly,** the **Angels** and Archangels, "the executors of the will **of** God throughout the universe," are **seen** nearest to **the** gospel-dome, standing above a rocky cave, in which are **three figures.** They appear to have various functions in the resurrection; the angel holds out a swathed man to **the** archangel, who holds a man (perhaps the same man),

* Mrs. Jameson's "Legendary Art," p. 45.

from whom the grave-clothes are falling. Between them they thus complete the resurrection of the dead.

It remains only for the visitor to observe, before leaving the chapel, the manner in which its different parts are related to each other. Upon the arch at the entrance to the gospel-dome are the Four Evangelists; on that which prefaces the altar-dome, with its display of heavenly triumph, are four saints "militant here on earth." But it is the domes themselves whose meaning is most evidently connected. In all, the same Figure is seen in the centre, surrounded in the first by the prophets of the Old Testament, in the second by the Apostles, in the third by the heavenly choirs, the three together thus proclaiming the promise, the ministry, and the triumph of the prophesied, crucified and glorified Christ.

SANCTUS, SANCTUS, SANCTUS,
DOMINUS, DEUS, OMNIPOTENS,
QUI ERAT, QUI EST, EST QUI VENTURUS EST.

Rev. iv. 8.

INDEX.

INDEX.

Birds, chased by Venetian boys, 63 ; legend of, and churches of Venice,
     2.
Bolton Abbey, 31.
Bribery, 71.
Brides of Venice, 1 S. 113.
British Museum, Cotton MS., pref. iv.
Buckle's civilization, 26.
Byzantine art, mythical, 90.
"   "   St. Mark's typical of, 78.
Byzantium conquered by Venice, 78.

Camerlenghi, treasurers of Venice, 26.
Cape of Good Hope, discovery of, ruins Venice, 28.
Capitals, laws of their treatment, 14. 17.
     "   of twelfth to fourteenth centuries, 14, 18.

10*